GOLDEN HARVEST

Goodly Heritage

GOLDEN HARVEST

Goodly Heritage

Rosanna C. Sharps

Word Sower Publishing

Book cover and interior design by Michael Sharps.

Printed in the United States of America

First Published 2021

ISBN: Softcover   978-1-7364833-7-4
          Hardcover   978-1-7364833-8-1
          eBook   978-1-7364833-9-8

Word Sower Publishing
Columbia, California

www.wordsowerpublishing.com

I would like to extend my gratitude to
those who assisted in my efforts in
publishing the "Golden Harvest Trilogy."

To God, for His inspiration.
To my husband, Michael for his support.
To Margaret, for providing the historical resources for Snelling.

Contents

1

Sower and Sons Farm

Early March 1875
Snelling, California

Jonathan Sower's saddle creaked as h adjusted himself on his dependable steed, Jake. The hazy morning sun's light filtered through the thin layer of mist left behind by the previous evening's chilled air. He and his horse's warm breath emit from their nostrils like steam from a simmering kettle when mingling with the cool atmosphere as they departed his well-established wheat ranch boasting 2,500 acres. The hearty country breakfast prepared by his domestic employee, Liang, liquefy in his stomach at a fast rate due to his bundled emotions in anticipation of the day's schedule. Possible confrontation scenarios with his new farm staff consumed his apperception as he headed toward his recent business acquisition, Sower and Sons Farm, on the southwest end of Snelling, once known as Maxfield Farm. A year shy of 50, his bones groaned like his aging saddle from his lifetime of back-breaking work in agriculture.

The past eleven years of hard labor on his land at Sower Farms is without any regret. The extensive acreage is more than he or his ancestors expected to own in their lifetime, and the good Lord continues to expand his vision and bless his business as the years progress. A sense of gratification filled Jonathan as he scanned the enormity of Sower Farms while trotting along the wayside path through the barren fields ready to be plowed.

Jonathan and his family made considerable advances since their departure from his father's farm in Kentucky to follow a God-given calling to move to California soon after his honorable discharge while serving in the Union army during the Civil War. If his father and grandfather were alive, they'd be proud of his accomplishments to complete a dream they both began. They ingrained into him the importance of family and their desire to pass on a heritage of wheat farming and land ownership to future Sower generations. His prayer is to instill the same aspiration in his children, and Lord willing, they with their own families.

The 2,500 acres of agricultural land Jonathan purchased in the northeastern region of Snelling surpassed his forefather's ambitions, and now another 3,500 acres await claim should Frederick Maxfield relinquish his life to illness with no one to inherit his achievements. Anguish impaled Jonathan for his ill-fated competitor when 1 Timothy 6:10 came to mind, '*For the love of money is the root of all evil: which while some coveted after, they have erred from the faith, and pierced themselves through with many sorrows.*' *Greed and wanting consumes that poor fellow. Money and fortune is his mistress, and he doesn't want to share her with anyone*'.

As Jonathan passed the schoolhouse and then the cemetery, he wondered about Maxfield's possible kinfolk. *He never married or bore children to inherit his estate. Nor does any living relatives exist to grieve him should he depart this world.*

The Snelling courthouse languished in the fresh morning dew as he traversed through town. The bank and vault, which provided a hefty loan for Maxfield to purchase his farm, share the first floor with the jail of the diversely utilized courthouse. Jonathan also recalled many early church gatherings on the second floor before the itinerant pastor had one built on Green Street.

Frederick is an indebted, miserable, hate-filled hermit with no one to love, not even God. I've never seen him in church or, at the least, socializing at the hotel's saloon. The community is small, and our acquaintances are the same. Without a doubt, someone shared the gospel with him on many occasions. Yet he keeps his distance.

Coming to the edge of town, he trod by the Chinese camp and the doctor's clinic. *Too bad Maxfield's prejudice toward our Asian brothers continues to blind him and cloud his reason. He could be widening his profit margin and improving his business practices by employing efficient farmhands and utilizing modern technology. No wonder he had a near-fatal stroke groveling over unnecessary evil vices.*

Jake snorted as they neared the former Maxfield Farm entrance. Samuel had removed the metal-plated sign bearing the previous business name, and only the brick side post and the iron gate remained. In due time after Jonathan purchases the property, he planned to install a new banner Sower and Sons Farm.

This land and the profit it used to make for the former wheat baron served his obsession, and his conniving reputation preceded it. So until Mr. Maxfield releases his holdings, I will not subject my name to his improper dealings. Other than leasing his lands, Frederick cannot claim any stakes in my business transactions. His circumstance is tragic, indeed. Now his misfortune is my gain. Not for me alone but for the love and security of my family and their children to come. My family's future is foremost on my heart. And there lies the difference between Maxfield and me ... our intentions. His is for selfish accrual, and mine for selfless benevolence.

The thickening grey clouds rumbled in the nearby Sierra Mountains. The horse's steady and confident gait depicted the seasoned wheat farmer's poise as they entered the grounds. Perplexed by surrealism, Jonathan tried embracing the fact he was now the grain industry tycoon in the San Joaquin Valley after acquiring the stroke-ridden mogul's business a few months earlier. He slapped his knee to assure this wasn't a dream.

Although Jonathan purchased his former competitor's wheat trade, which included the crops, the livestock, the outdated farm equipment, and the overpaid employees, the complete sense of entitlement escaped him since the land was still under Maxfield's holding. He leased the acreage from the ailing land baron. Also excluded in the agreement is the farmhouse, which Frederick still resided until his dying day.

Jonathan would not allow this atypical agronomical approach to buck him from his saddle. He understood the wheat industry inside and out and was able to maneuver about the business with his eyes closed and hands lassoed behind his back. Working around a malefic land baron is an experience he is yet to encounter.

Looming in Jonathan's plans is to transition into a different agricultural commodity known only by him and his immediate family for the newly acquired second farm. The fruit and nut commerce required his consideration as the demand intensified in the blossoming Western economy.

These God-given visionary talents air strong in the Sower bloodline, establishing his grandfather in Virginia, his father at his homestead in Kentucky, and himself and his family at their current location in the burgeoning California frontier. He recognized this distinction in his four children, in particular, his eldest son, Samuel. He only needed to keep him pointed in the right direction so he may one day receive the bulk of the inheritance.

Now that Samuel is married I hope he'll come home with shouts of joy and bring in the sheaves with his wife. I must increase his responsibilities when he and Jia-Li return from their honeymoon.

Jonathan craned his neck as he scanned the immense acreage. The land stretched further than his own into a region neighboring the next county. A sudden pang of anxiety pressed his chest, overwhelmed by the gravity of the takeover.

Tumbling through his mind were the financial statements and budget scenarios provided by his second daughter, Naomi, a few weeks earlier. After lumbering and praying over the numbers, both he and his wife, Mary, decided to maintain the 2500 acre wheat crop at Sower Farm, but transition into the sought after fruit and nut industry at Sower and Sons Farm. Samuel and Lad, the husband of his eldest daughter, Sarah, would manage the second location, and his Chinese supervisors oversee the first. Upon his youngest son's return from seminary and aside from ministry, David could assist Naomi with the financial matters.

Where would I be without my family to partner with in managing two major agricultural enterprises? The timing is divine. Had this opportunity occurred a year or two ago when my adult children had issues of their own to overcome, I wouldn't have given business expansion a second thought because of the lack of support I would need to succeed.

Jonathan shaded his eyes and sharpened his focus as far as his sight would allow, imagining the colossal task of planting almond and peach trees. The pounding of his heart pulsated to the base of his head at a dizzying rate. Nausea followed, but then the Lord's small still voice within him intervened and quoted Deuteronomy 31:6 to bring comfort and calm.

'Be strong and of a good courage, fear not, nor be afraid of them: for the LORD thy God, he is that doth go with thee; he will not fail thee, nor forsake thee.'

Jonathan inhaled the moistened air from the incoming rain, then dismounted by the gated entrance to pray before entering the grounds. He fell to his knees, grabbed a handful of soil, and held it before the Lord.

"Dear God, I am so undeserving of such great responsibility. You continue to open doors of opportunity to me beyond my comprehension and abilities, and more than doubled the size of my holdings. I pray I can meet your expectations. For that, I am exceedingly grateful, and I trust Your judgment.

"Thank You, Lord, for leading my eldest son and daughter home and drawing them back to You and the vision You created for our kinfolk here in Snelling. I pray You would protect Samuel and his wife Jia-Li, and continue to strengthen Sarah and Lad's family and their children, Amanda, Billy, and especially Isabel. As for Naomi, Lord, I hope you find her the proper husband, one who can appreciate and love her inner beauty and abilities. And for David, give him the wisdom needed to fulfill his callin' and a spouse who would love and encourage him as well. Lord, I thank You most of all for my beautiful and excellent wife, Mary. Bless her with Your abundant grace for her patience and everlastin' support of the dream You gave us despite past hardships and the ones yet to come with this new endeavor at Sower and Sons Farm.

"Lord, this takeover will be a challenge, indeed. I pray for your blessings upon this land now under my care. The conversion of produce does not trouble me as much as what festers inside this farm's barn. It could make or break this reverie. From the report Samuel and Lad provided, S&S Farm will require major overhaulin' to obtain the height of glory You desire. I trust in You and the vision You planted in my heart many years ago. Lord, please provide strength and wisdom to fulfill your will in my life with assistance from family and employees. Thank you for Your mercy and grace. Prepare the way before me, oh Lord, and I will follow!"

2

Change

Four sets of egregious eyes ensued Jonathan's every movement as he and Lad, the head livestock supervisor, perused S&S Farm's senescent barn. Heavy raindrops splattered on the tin roof as the caliginous cloud's silver jagged lightning strikes lit the dim and dusty building's interior through the shuttered window cracks. Avoiding contention, Jonathan muzzled his disappointed thoughts, allowing a grunt or two to escape his survey of the aging livestock and farm equipment.

Jonathan's son, Samuel, the newly appointed head foreman of S&S Farm, was assigned the difficult task of discussing with the former Maxfield employees the plans to update the farming equipment and techniques utilized by the previous owner. However, his son's wedding plans took precedence over conveying Jonathan's detailed vision for the second farm. With the wedding celebration behind them and while his son and daughter-in-law are away on honeymoon, Jonathan hoped to convene the second farm's oversight and become acquainted with his added staff.

Acquiring Maxfield's wheat business so close to the next planting season gave Jonathan no other choice but to employ Harold, Leonard, Grier, and Nevil. He needed their existing farming equipment knowledge and expertise to circumvent financial loss in the first year of acquisition.

Maxfield and his former employees had made known that they detested Sower Farms for their enterprising business philosophies, in particular, the employment of the more affordable, reliable, and efficient Chinese labor. The completion of the American transcontinental railroad deserted many of these men, leaving them scrambling for any work they could find. Indubitably, the Chinese were favored by most farmers, including Jonathan, leaving many white workers with ill sentiments toward the invading Celestials.

Job security restrains these former Maxfield employees from boiling over and exploding under Jonathan's management. He must express his vision for this farm, and these men must accept it if they are to remain in his employ. The changes may be their tipping point, so he must tread with caution, and keep the situation under control.

"You fellows appear to be on top of things. The livestock and equipment seem to be in order considerin' their antiquity," Jonathan said as he, Lad, and the four farmhands settled themselves on hay bales. The men sat with crossed arms while chewing tobacco loaded in their cheek. An occasional lightning flash outside brightened the barn's interior, intensifying their rugged features for a brief moment. Their dusty straw hats tilt to the back of their heads, clearing their view of him, the new auger. The dirt ground into their clothing and hands revealed the years of arduous labor they've encountered working the fields.

Harold spat on the ground. "Yes, sir. Did you doubt our abilities?"

"No. Not at all. Part of Maxfield's success was because you men were good at what you do. He's been doin' business as long, if not longer than me." Jonathan stood and paced, staring at his boots, choosing his words, and hoping his praiseworthy comments would alleviate the escalating animosity. "Misfortune never crops up at a proper time. However, for Maxfield, it couldn't have occurred durin' a better season. To keep with the competition, he would've had to replace the existin' equipment as I've done, which takes some alterations and financial plannin'. Perhaps he realized his poor health would limit him, and maybe that's why he never got around to doin' it."

Maxfield would've had to lay off half his men with the new equipment. I'm sure that's his secondary reasonin' for not movin' forward. Sometimes one has to cut off the fat to enjoy the best portion of the steak. Tellin' these men the truth will cause more trouble than I bargained for right now. That'll happen soon enough when I have firm control of S&S Farm.

Jonathan paused, shoved his hands in his pant pockets, and made eye contact with the men. "My last harvest proved the efficiency of new technology as I was able to go to market far sooner than my competitors. My plan for this farm is to not only update the farmin' equipment with the profits gained this season…" he inhaled, turned toward the barn door, and blurted out his vision before ambivalence changed his mind, "…but also transition the crops into almond and peach groves within the next five years."

There. I've said it. Things are about to change, whether they like it or not. He crossed his arms and turned to observe their reactions.

The four men jerked back as if Jonathan's fist swung at them. Harold stood, chest protruding like an angry cock, and positioned himself within spitting range of Jonathan. Fire flashed eyes and clenched hands, he snarled. "Over my dead body, you will. Maxfield won't allow you to do such a thing."

Jonathan huffed as his son-in-law stood behind him. "We'll soon see about that." He held his chin high. "Maxfield has no say in *my* business decisions. There were no clauses in our contract as to how this land is to be utilized by the lessee." Jaw clamped, Jonathan held his ground and returned a stabbing glare. "As I see it, you can walk out that door and not deal with the changes, or you can take a seat and work with me."

All breathing in the barn, livestock included, seemed to stop as the focus fell on Harold. Undefined words sputtered through his thinned lips as his hands balled into a fist.

The anticipation of a blowing strike from the disgruntled employee caused Jonathan's body to tense. No doubt, the other men would follow their leader like meat bees on defenseless prey. Harold's decision would determine him and his men's survival in an employment lacking economy outnumbered by the growing western population.

Curses spewed from Harold's mouth as his chest decompressed, much like a locomotive would open its safety valve when letting out built-up steam. He lowered his glare, slammed his right fist into his left palm, and returned to his seat. The room breathed again.

After the men had settled down, Jonathan grasped his hands behind him and continued. "When plantin' begins, I want each of you men to take turns bein' trained on the new equipment by my staff at Sower Farm."

"What? Now you expect us to bow down to a bunch of Coolies! You might as well throw us to the swine." Harold growled.

"Yep. I expect that and more if you claim to be as good as you say. You should be able to implement this equipment more rapidly than your Asian counterparts and prove to me your worth keepin'." A smirk escaped him as he moved toward Lad. *Things are goin' to get real interestin' watchin' these boys workin' with my Chinese staff. It'll be like oil and water. The two won't mix.*

At the barn door, Jonathan filled his lungs with fresh, moist air. "All right. The season begins when Sam returns from his honeymoon in a couple of weeks. Decide amongst yourself who'll report to me first."

THE FOUR MEN INSTIGATED among themselves as Jonathan and Lad shuffled out the barn and headed for home.

"Dang if I'm going to let that auger change anything 'round here. We'll have to add some fat to the fire and frustrate his plans a bit." Harold adjusted the chew with his tongue, then spat on the ground.

"Whew. For sure I thought you were goin' to slog the ol' man one," Grier said, air boxing.

Leonard pulled a straw from the hay bale and shoved it in his mouth to gnaw on. "You had me rattled for a moment, Harold. I thought I'd have to become a chuck-line-rider if you chose to cut a path out that door. Gossiping from ranch to ranch for a meal would not go down well with my rib. Evelyn is content with her wifely duties to an alfalfa desperado."

Neville hee-hawed. "Well, Harold. Since you're the top ranny amongst us, what are your plans to put a spoke in our new auger's wheel? And who are you goin' to send first to work with them Celestials?"

"Now you hay shakers don't go havin' a conniption fit. Yeah, I'll go first so I can examine the lay-of-the-land if you know what I mean."

Harold stood, eyes focused on the barn door. "The first thing I'm going to do is to meet at the farmhouse with ol' boss Maxfield and let him know about Sower's plans. I'm sure it'll make him as mad as a March hare. He'll probably have some ideas of his own. He may not own the business anymore, but he still holds this land. He'll want to know what's happening to it." Harold winked at the men and skedaddled out the door toward Maxfield's farmhouse.

"I'LL K...K...KILL 'EM. KILL 'EM." Frederick Maxfield's rounded eyes met Harold's. "Nuh, nuh, nuh." Slurring sounds spewed from his lips drooping side as his body convulsed on his bed from the disturbing news Harold delivered.

"I'm here, sir." The nurse held the stricken man's shaking hand while she pulled a handkerchief from her white apron pocket and wiped the drool off his chin. Her fingers rested on his wrist to check his pulse rate. "Mr. Maxfield, you need to calm down so I can give you your medicine. Come on now. Breathe in slow. Now exhale. Breathe in." Her voice spewed commands like a staff sergeant. She paused a second. "Now exhale. Again."

As Maxfield's body began to relax, and the convulsions dissipate, the nurse tucked the sheets around her patient and repositioned his head on his pillows. She then tugged at the white cuffs of her dark day dress, fluffed the ruffles on her white cap, then pulled Harold outside of the bedroom to give him strict instructions.

"Sir, I'm going to have to ask you to leave unless you want to cause this man another stroke." She wagged her finger under Harold's scruffy nose and overgrown mustache. "Frankly, I don't think he'll survive another episode."

"It's in his best interest to be aware of what's happening to his property," Harold whispered with urgency in his voice. His knees shook at the half-pint commando with sharp glaring eyes. *She must've served in the Civil War amongst cantankerous soldiers to develop such a strict steely character.*

"No, sir. What matters to this man is that the rent is paid on time to pay for his medical bills. For this reason, he sold the business ... to get out from under it. Please, you mustn't bother him with this news again. The matter is out of his hands and in yours now. You heard what he said. Now, if you'll excuse me, I must administer his medicine." The nurse turned on her heels and returned to Maxfield's room, leaving Harold dumbfounded.

Well, I know Fred's position in this matter better than that nurse does, and he wouldn't stand for Sower's plan. In fact, his last words were 'kill them.' Take matters into my hands; I will. I'll show Sower who the best hay shakers are. No Coolies are going to get the better of my men and me. Don't you worry ol' boss, I've got your back.

3

A Blissful Tide

Sandalwood, with a touch of English clove, rose, citrus and cedarwood perfume lingered on the soft curvature of Samuel's bride's slender neck, shoulders, and back as she lay enveloped in his arms in bed after the evening's romantic interlude. The light touch of his fingertips trailing down Jia-Li's spine aroused her from her sleep as her long dark silken strands caressed his cheek. She writhed beneath his touch as she reached for his face and drew close to kiss his lips.

Morning light drifted in through the window's thin curtains in the borrowed apartment at San Francisco's China Town. Jia- Li's father had made reservations with a merchant acquaintance to rent the one-bedroom flat for the newlywed's honeymoon suite. This arrangement deemed appropriate for the interracial couple rather than entangling themselves in disapproving confrontations with prejudicial clerks and hotel regulations.

Samuel and Jia-Li planned to keep a low profile while on their honeymoon to escape any discriminatory actions bent toward them. No amount of hostility would detract them from enjoying their heaven infused moment together. As husband and protector, Samuel would do anything to guard his precious gift from the scorn of animosity. His immense love for her would brave all odds to keep them bound to one another.

"Good morning, my love." Samuel groaned. His hands caressed her above her lacy chemise. The tingling sensation of his touch caused her back to arch and press against his body. Soon their bodies were as one moving together like the ocean's waves surging into the bay's open shores. The harmony of their love song crescendo to the heights of euphoria, sending them to an enchanted place only lovers can know. He adored her with a passion, unlike he's felt before. Moments like this would fill the remainder of his days, and he was well pleased.

Pushing aside the entangled sheets, she stretched herself atop him. "What is your bidding today, my husband?" Jia-Li wrinkled her nose and let out a sultry giggle. "Besides making love all night and day, we've got to eat sometime to keep up our strength. I'm starving. How about some breakfast, then we explore San Francisco? We are on our honeymoon, after all."

AFTER A SIMPLE MORNING MEAL of hard-boiled egg and fresh fruit, the newlyweds donned their coats and, with childlike eagerness, departed their nest to discover the grandeur of the metropolitan city. Once known as a sleepy settlement village called Yerba Buena, when first recognized in the early 19th century by the Englishman, William Richardson, its population comprised of a mere 800 Mexicans, Indians, and early pioneers. The discovery of gold in December 1848 drew fortune finders from around the globe. They arrived in droves by wagon train across the continent and tall ships docking in San Francisco Bay, which increased the populous to over 25,000 in 1849. The completed transcontinental railway in 1869 aided in the population boom, and now the city boasted a multitude of well over 150,000 people. Victorian-style buildings graced the steep, narrow streets, horse and carriage carted passengers to and fro, the bay teamed with white mast ships carrying the world's goods, and a brand new cable car climbed its way to the star lined hilltop horizon of the bustling city.

The newlyweds meandered through the crowded, steeply graded

streets by horsecar on steel rails and visited several tourist sites. They toured Mision de San Francisco de Assis on 16ᵗʰ Street, purchased chocolate confections at Mrs. Ghirardelli & Company on Greenwich and Powell Street, rode the brand new cable car from the top of Nob Hill down Clay Street, and headed toward the fisherman's wharf to sample the delectable Dungeness crab.

"I'll take two plates of the cooked crab and two sourdough bread and clam chowder bowls, please," said Samuel handing the vendor money as his partner stirred an enormous steaming pot of boiled crab behind him.

"Please take a seat inside and get out of the cold. I'll bring your order to you," said the vendor pointing at the small restaurant with dark cedar walls, floors, and tables nestled along the pier beside other fish markets and small restaurants. He winked at Samuel and slid in a crooked grin at Jia-Li.

"Thank you, sir." Samuel placed his hand on Jia-Li's waist and whispered in her ear. "Let's go inside, my love before this buffoon gets any more strange ideas about us."

They tried their best to avoid the judgmental gawkers and their snide remarks towards their mixed relationship. In most places, onlookers seemed to label Jia-Li as a Chinese prostitute and him as an eccentric immoral businessman. However, in this bustling multi-cultural seaport city, some were too busy to notice. It was the ideal honeymoon location for a Caucasian man married to an Asian beauty.

They scurried inside the noisy, cramped room. People of different ethnic backgrounds crowded on bench tables, smacked their lips as they cracked open the crab bodies, suckled on its tender meat, and slurped down the hot creamy clam chowder. Some seats became available as others finished their meal, deposited their trash in bins, and left the room.

"Where would you like to sit, darlin'? There's a seat by that older couple over there or by those Chinese fellows in that corner?" Samuel glanced at both tables.

Jia-Li's face turned a sheepish color.

Samuel clutched her hand. "Are you all right, my love?"

She inhaled. "Yes, yes. I'll be fine. I guess I'd rather sit by that old couple and deal with their remarks than sit by those men who look to me like they may cause us trouble and recruit me in their prostitution ring." Gulping hard, she squeezed Sam's hand as they approached the old couple.

"Hello. May we share your table?" Samuel asked.

Two wrinkled Caucasian faces peered up at them. The woman let out a gasp and shuffled her feet, kicking her husband's foot, and the old man clenched his spoon, cleared his throat and glared at Samuel. "I suppose so." Spit splattered from his lips amongst his thick Irish accent. "We're just about to leave anyway." He turned to his wife, who grunted and squinted at him.

"Thank you."

No sooner after Samuel and Jia-Li sat, the elderly couple gathered their belongings and dismissed themselves. The vendor approached with their food and placed it before them. The hot steamy seafood aroma drifted about their faces, and they plunged into the delicious feast.

Adoring his wife's beauty, fearful thoughts of imprisonment lingered because of California's anti-miscegenation laws. He loved and adored Jia-Li, and nothing could tear him away from her. Had it not been for Pastor McSwan's un-discriminatory views toward the Chinese and the fact that Jia-Li's family were Christians, he and Jia-Li would not have been married by the compassionate clergyman in the church. Obtaining a marriage license with the state of California would be he and Jia-Li's most significant obstacle. He pushed the thought aside. *We'll get our marriage license in Texas or Mexico if we have to. I'll deal with that later or maybe not at all and remain quiet. Jia-Li and I are the least of the sheriff's worries. They have far greater problems in this lawless state to keep them busy.*

THE NEWLYWEDS spent the remaining two weeks navigating through the city's Asian section filled with fresh fish markets, Chinese herbal apothecary stores, kitchenware and garment shops, and best of all, an abundance of restaurants where Samuel and Jia-Li ate all of the Asian delicacies to their heart's content. For Samuel, the unusual blended scents of fresh seafood, herbs, spices, and a hint of ocean breeze wafting through the air added to the unique ambiances of the growing cosmopolitan city.

Although he was savoring every moment spent with his new bride, Samuel could not help but also worry about the considerable undertaking his father and brother-in-law were regulating while he was away from Sower and Sons Farm. He knew that the inherited Maxfield assistant supervisors were very difficult men. The new change of industry from wheat to fruits and nuts would certainly ruffle the new employee's feathers. Samuel could only imagine what trouble lay ahead for his family. They alone could not handle the dastardly deeds these four men concocted. But his father had no choice but to use those men because of the timing of acquiring the second farm.

Samuel knew his father counted on all the Sower households, including his younger brother, David, upon his return from college to help manage the farm's business affairs. His sisters and mother would assist with the administrative duties, maintain the family garden and fruit trees behind the farmhouse, and his wife's family would continue to attend to both the family's domestic needs. The farm's matters clouded his mind interrupting his honeymoon's pleasantries. His heart desired to remain in this blissful tide, yet his spirit invoked urges to go home and confront the difficulties ahead of him.

4

Dirty Deed

Perched on the Standish Mayflower steam traction engine's driver seat, which pulled a plow with ten bottoms in the field closest Sower Farm's barn, the lead superintendent, Ah Yung cringed after he detected a lone rider approaching from the far end of the wayside path. He expelled savory Mandarin words as his cohorts, Ah Sheng-Li and Ah Anguo, stood beside him with long faces. The seasoned Asian superintendents dreaded the assignment given them to train their rival enemies, the old Maxfield employees, now under Jonathan Sower's management since the takeover.

The misty cold morning air combined with the engine's warm breath produced a dense cloud bath which enveloped the nearby landscape. A shivering ache arrested Ah Yung's chest as the devilish white superintendent from S&S Farm immerged from the eerie haze. "Hold your tongues, brothers, and help me to do the same. The next four weeks working with this cowboy and his subordinates will be hell. Let's train them then send them back to S&S Farm." He pulled a rag from his trouser pocket and began wiping the condensation on the engine's gears.

The two assistant superintendents locked their jaws and released hot gasps between their teeth, much like the plumes of smoke billowing from the engine's stack. Ah Anguo tossed a few more logs into the firebox and used a poker to arrange them for maximum burning efficiency then closed the damper. "If I had no respect for Mr. Jonathan, I would tell him that I refuse to associate with Mr. Maxfield's evil employees. But I regard him with great honor for choosing us to work for him when other farmers would not give us one ounce of their favor."

Ah Sheng-Li pat Ah Anguo's shoulder as if to calm him, then checked the engine's gages. "Well, they are Mr. Jonathan's employees now, and we must comply." He opened the cylinder drain cocks. "Yes, I would like to do the same. But we know our place. Besides, Mr. Jonathan is aware of the contentions between them and us. Just be thankful training them is only for this season. Next year they are on their own." The men grunted in agreement with the thought.

"Let's just do our best so that we stand blameless, men," Ah Yung said. "In due time, their wicked nature will be found out."

Dismounting, Howard tied his horse's reign to the fence post and moseyed over to the field. His cocky physique dwarfed as he stood beside the labor-saving and scale-intensive new farming technology's massive thick, treaded traction wheels.

Ah Yung smirked at the change of tides. Now he held the superior reins over this white superintendent who once hurled derogatory remarks at Chinese laborers when boarding Jonathan and Samuel's work wagons in town during past seasons. Exercising his authority, Ah Yung sat straight, puffed out his chest, and sneered down his nose at the demoted farmhand standing below him.

Hands firm on his hips, Harold then tipped his straw hat and glared up at the Sower Farm superintendents. "All right. Let's get this week over with. I know y'all dislike my company as I do yours. Show me what I need to do with this contraption." He spat on the ground and pulled on his work gloves from inside his dusty suede coat.

"Climb on board, Mr. Howard." Ah Yung snarled. "The ladder is on the other side." He turned around and rolled his eyes. This week is going to be long and stressful.

FRUSTRATION PEAKED after Harold worked five ten-hour days with the people he most detested, and became overwhelmed by the complicated modern farming inventions. This system was far more advanced than the outdated equipment his previous employer and his cohorts were using. Implementing this method would require less human and animal labor, reduce cost, increase productivity, and save time. The scarcity of jobs will cause an outcry amongst the white farmworkers knowing they have to compete with these Celestials. Now he understood, but would never openly agree with Jonathan Sowers' plans to make changes to Maxfield's old deteriorating methods. For the wheat business to survive, advancements must be made even at the expense of laying off employees. A most precarious situation for farm owners indeed.

As the sun settled on the horizon, the Chinese superintendents directed the steam traction engine back to the barn. Standing in the rear of the cab envying the fluid and well-coordinated quality of his rivals, Howard pushed his straw hat back and scratched his head as he calculated numbers in his mind. Well, if I ain't a monkey's uncle. We just plowed 400 acres in a week using one locomotive and three men and will furrow all 2500 acres in six weeks at this rate. This amount of land would've taken almost six months to plow with Maxfield's ten horses and plows and a dozen farmworkers. No wonder Sower beat us to market every time. This method is five times faster and more efficient. These scrawny Chinamen are stronger and smarter than they appear too. My men would be bitchin' and complainin' by now. Anger and jealousy rumbled in his belly. I can't let this happen; it's either these Coolies or us. California is my home now, and we've taken it fair and square from the Mexicans and Indians. I'm not about to let some foreign invaders take what is mine. They can take their celestial know-how and go back to where they came from.

The engine outside the barn, Ah Sheng-Li leaned out the cab window after he opened the valve to blow down the boiler. The loud hissing sound of released steam interrupted Howard's train of thought. Closing the damper, Ah Anguo put down the fire. Both men grabbed oil cans, climbed down the engine, and began oiling the moving parts.

"Do you have any questions?" Ah Yung asked.

"Uh … no," Howard said too proud to admit his confusion. "I'm sure it'll all make sense once Mr. Sower purchases an engine for S&S Farm."

Ah Yung nodded his head, although his expression displayed disdain.

"Leonard will join you next week. I'll be sure he takes good notes." Howard climbed down the ladder, hurled spit on the ground, and dismissed himself without showing any signs of gratitude. *Now, if only I can get my men to work as diligent as these Chinamen, we'd have them beat.* He mounted his horse and headed for his home in town.

SOWER FARM LAY PLACID shrouded in the evening's fog induced darkness after six weeks of plowing under tense conditions. Harold, Leonard, Grier, and Nevil trained one week each in succession with the Chinese superintendents. After the men turned the fields, they readied the broadcast boxes to be used for the month of sowing starting the following week. Outside of the barn, large crates of durum wheat seed were placed side-by-side, waiting to be planted. Jonathan's grandfather brought this heritage brand seed to America at the turn of the 19th century from their ancestral lands in Europe, and it thrived in the rich cultivated California soil. A long weekend of rest began for the farmhands that evening before undertaking the next step in the planting season.

Nestled inside the farmhouse, the grandfather clock resounded in the candlelit foyer as its pendulum ticked and tocked. With the first quarter of the new planting season completed, the Sower household rested their heads on their pillows in anticipation of the second quarter's seed sowing. Both farms tracked on schedule according to the resources and abilities of each location, Sower Farm months ahead of Sower and Sons Farm.

NOT ONE STAR SHONE through the midnight's heavy Tule fog, which immersed Snelling and the San Joaquin Valley floor. Moisture from the periodic rain showers condensed into a thick cloud from the night's rapid cooling, leaving zero visibility. Only the sound of the livestock lowing and the Merced River's rushing waters less than a mile away from Sower Farm penetrated the opaque night air.

Four horses and two masked riders dressed in shady clothing lurked about the thickening fog behind the barn. The moistened ground absorbed the sound of the horse's hooves. They stopped where the crates stood. Both culprits dismounted and crept about the large containers of durum with stealth.

"Quick. Grab the other corner and let's remove the canvas," the lead deviant whispered as the other grunted and followed suit unveiling the opened mouth wooden boxes laden with wheat seed.

Pulling the sacks of darnel seeds from the back of the other two horses, the villainous intruders used their buck knives for ripping them open and began mixing the tare with the wheat.

"Sure glad we can finally put this bad grain to use. I was wonderin' why you had us keep them."

"I figured these weeds would come in handy one day. Sower won't realize what happened to his precious crop until it's too late. If they want to pluck out the darnel, they'd have to destroy some of the wheat along with it. And you know he won't allow that to happen.

"All right. You start at one end, and I'll begin on the other. Let's work fast and skedaddle out of here before we get caught."

After finishing their dirty deed, they recovered the canvas, gathered the empty sacks, mounted their steeds, and with covertness guided all four animals away from Sower Farms. They disappeared into the night's blackness the same as they had entered, being careful to leave no evidence of their corruption.

5

Proposal

The ushers opened the front doors as the pastor dismissed the congregation at the Church of Christ on the Forks of Little Buck Creek in Indiana. The women chattered and tee-heed as they greeted one another, their bright floral bonnets accenting their full-flowing pastel day dresses. The men followed the course in their dapper suits and beaver pelt hats as the children in their Sunday best bolted outside with shouts of glory eager to enjoy the sunshine. David attended service with the Harrington Family and Catherine's wealthy city-dwelling brother, Hudson Wilcox, Esquire, and his wife, Alice, who came to visit on the highly significant day of Christian observance. The crisp spring air and clear blue skies mimic the joy which filled David's heart that morning in anticipation of his announcement planned later that day.

Gathering on the church's front lawn sprinkled with white-winged butterflies flitting about the brilliant yellow daisy hedges, David struck up a light conversation. "Moderator Parr delivered an appropriate gospel message for this glorious Easter mornin'. Nothing better than a fiery salvation message to stir a sinner's conviction, repentance, and bring them to their knees to ask for forgiveness from the Almighty Father. The Spirit continues to move my heart to preach the gospel to the lost."

"Yes, indeed. Our family began attending this church about five years ago. It's the closest one to our home," Clarence, David's college roommate, said, shaking his head. "Although, I'm not quite in agreement with the Baptists' predestination doctrine and that God pre-determines whom He desires to save."

"Now, son, let's not get started on that now," Clayton, Clarence's father, said. "For the sake of our small community's many denominational backgrounds, the moderators have agreed to preach on the essentials of salvation during Sunday services to maintain the spirit of worship amongst its visitors. Those desirous of the Baptists' Calvinist teachings are invited to attend other meetings during the week."

"And now you can understand why I am attending seminary. My calling is to plant a church having Wesleyan doctrine in our growing township," Clarence's face glowed as he stopped and lay his hand on David's shoulder. "I sure could use the assistance of someone with the same vision to partner with me in this mission."

"Oh, David, wouldn't that be wonderful if you assist my brother in such a grand endeavor. This little town of Marion is about to become a major hub once the gas industries start building. Our town will need more churches." Clara bat her thick lashes, which framed her green eyes that shimmered above her magnetic smile as she stood beside him. Warmth emanated from her parent's disposition as they returned radiant beams at him and Clara. The young couple had officially made known to the family of their courtship the previous Christmas.

David's knees buckled, his eyelids fluttered, and his jaw dropped. "I, I, I."

No, this is not what God is calling me to do. What should I say to them? Lord, You know I love Clara and plan on asking for her hand in marriage today. She knows my heart is to minister to the communities in my hometown of Snelling, especially to the Chinese. Oh Lord, I don't want to break the hearts of this family, which I've come to love as my own. Is this another door You are openin' for me, Lord? What do You want me to do?

Without delay, God bestowed David's lips with wisdom and grace. "Your calling is marvelous, my brother. I will certainly have to pray about your proposition. I'll bring your request before the Lord. If God desires to change His plans for me to minister to the Chinese immigrants in California and stay here to assist you, then I'm sure He'll give me a vision and confirm my new calling in His word." David shook Clarence's hand and nodded with assurance at the Harrington family.

As if commiserating with David's dilemma, Hudson interrupted. "Perhaps you would consider praying for a more affluent and stable occupation in law as I have, David," he grunted tugging at his cuffs and distributing his robust weight upon his elaborate gold-handled walking stick, "to provide for your future family. Have you considered the effects of their economy while you pursue a minister's lowly existence?"

Did their uncle, Hudson Wilcox, attorney of law, snub me and his nephew's benevolent province? Perhaps his purpose for visiting his sister and her family is to save his niece by discouraging our relationship and prohibiting her from becoming a minister's wife. Since his spouse is unable to bear children, he must feel entitled to overseeing his younger sister's children as his own. Does he resent his sister marrying a simple country farmer with a livery stable? Well, he'll have two ministers in the family and a brother-in-law to temper his arrogance.

Catherine's face flushed at her brother's snobbish remark. "Humble. You mean humble existence, Hudson." Not allowing him another word, she turned to David and Clarence. "Well, why don't we discuss these callings over an Easter luncheon? Shall we head back to our home?" She extended her hand to her husband, and the family boarded their wagon.

CLARA STOOD TO CLEAR THE DINING TABLE after everyone had finished consuming the ham and sweet potato lunch. Without hesitating, David tugged at her hand and motioned her to sit down as he rose to clink his glass to gain the family's attention. The moment arrived, which he prepared for and envisioned since he and Clara's courtship. An emotional bundle wedged itself at his throat's threshold. However, an overwhelming determination managed to push through the obstruction. With Clayton and Catherine in full focus, David searched his mind for his rehearsed lines.

"Mr. and Mrs. Harrington, I hope you won't mind me taking a few moments of your time to share my gratitude and personal hope and vision for the future. First, I want to begin by saying how grateful I am for your most gracious hospitality since arriving here in Indiana. I thank the Lord for His divine orchestration in choosing Clarence as my roommate and stepping stone to meeting all of you. Your love and friendship is blessing me and providing a pleasant distraction from the bombardment of my collegiate studies. I look forward to spending my school breaks here with your family."

David loosened his cravat and turned, "My greatest source of inspiration, next to the Lord Himself, is and will continue to be your beautiful daughter, Clara. My spirit leaped with joy when I first laid eyes on her. I believe in my heart that God has guided me here to equip me for His calling in my life. Not only with His wisdom and knowledge, but also with the support I would need from, I pray, my future wife and her family."

Pausing, David viewed his audience for reactionary signs. At the table's head, Clayton sat erect and grasped his chair's arms. At the other end, Hudson frowned as Alice held her breath. A nervous grin crossed Catherine's face as she wrung her cloth napkin on her lap. Brows raised, Clarence grimaced, winked, and gave a thumbs up. The youngest, Cora, wiggled and giggled in her seat. And Clara. Her adoring eyes and warm smile melted his heart like butter on a hot summer day.

David fell to one knee and reached inside his coat's pocket and pulled out a simple gold band. "Clara, will you marry this humble aspiring minister?"

Clara gasped, and joyful tears trickled to her radiant smile. "Yes, David. I would be honored to be your wife."

David turned to her parents. "Mr. and Mrs. Harrington. May I have your permission to wed your daughter, Clara?"

Clayton extended his hand to his wife as she nodded at him. They locked eyes with David and, in unison, said, "Yes, you may."

"We couldn't be more blessed to have you as our son-in-law, David," Clayton said.

As David held Clara's hand, he slipped the band onto her left ring finger and stood. "Not a day goes by that I find myself drifting from my studies thinking about you, my darlin'. Having marital love and assurance will reinforce the drive I need to press forward in my God-ordained destiny." He turned to the family. "Our hope is to be married this August before the fall semester begins. I pray that date will also meet your approval."

Catherine recited the months as she counted on her fingers. "We have six months to plan. That should be plenty of time to prepare a beautiful country wedding." She turned to her husband. "Wouldn't it, dear?"

"More than enough," Clayton said while he slapped his knee. "Just let us know what you both desire, and your mother and I will do our best to accommodate you. We are so happy for you both."

All at the table cheered, except for Hudson, whose face turned red with anger, and his glassy eyes sent flaming darts at David.

6

Beauty

An envelope with David's return address caught Naomi's eye as she shuffled through the stack of mail on the secretary's roll-top desk in her father's farmhouse office. Letter in hand, she whisked over to her mother, who sat by the hearth knitting as her father sat across reading the San Joaquin Argus.

"Ma, a letter from David." Naomi handed the envelope to Mary and sat down, waiting for news of his spiritual journey at a faraway place east of California. Although Indiana rested in the Midwestern region of the United States, she envisioned it as a distant territory since the young country fell shy of its 100th anniversary as a nation with locations yet to be discovered. Land grabs, gold, and new inventions ushered in a mass population increase. People raced across the country in search of property ownership, opportunity, and fortune at the expense of the original inhabitants and those who may interfere in one's progress. Until state and federal officials established laws in the new territories, many of its citizens performed self-imposed regulations utilizing the justice of a firing arm. Excitement and danger raged in pioneering hearts.

Naomi lived vicariously through her sibling's adventures outside of Snelling. Samuel, when he left home for his gold panning expedition in the motherlode, then as a railroad worker laying track in the high

Sierras and Nevada desert. Also, through her eldest sister, Sarah, and her turbulent life with her cow wrangling husband and their three adorable children as they braved mountain living in Mariposa. Now through her young brother, who traveled the country by train to educate himself for a relentless calling to preach the gospel to the Chinese who relocated to California in search of Gam Saan, or Gold Mountain.

Although her siblings would scarcely acknowledge their lives as accomplished, Naomi admired their courage to try new experiences even if it included the possibility of failure or dislike. Their attempt is better than not trying at all and removes all their wondering and wanting. Courage and strength dominate the main characteristics of the Sower clan. Her parents sat contented before her in the comforts of their beloved farmhouse and homestead because they risked all odds to follow their heart to California. Is their dream my future too, Lord? As much as I love my family and this farm, will this be all there is to my life? What opportunities and aspirations lay before me? What is my calling?

Unlike her brothers and sister, nothing drew her to leave the comforts of home. Everything she needed and wanted lay in the vast property her parents acquired, and so she thought. She hoped to one day inherit even a portion of their wealth. Why her siblings desired something else baffled her.

Her mother adjusted her spectacles and began reading to herself when her hands and lips began to quiver.

"Oh my, Lord," Mary said, her mouth agape. "My youngest is engaged!"

The wall of newspaper collapsed on her father's lap, and he peered over his reading glasses. "What? No," he said half-grinning. "Our boy popped the question, did he now?" He snapped his finger. "I hope the lucky gal is Clara, his roommate's sister."

"She is darlin'. And they planned their weddin' date for this August before the fall semester. Preparations have begun, and they want our entire family to attend."

"Well, of course, we will. Lord, I hope she is everything we prayed for. David will need a wife with spiritual strength and measurable faith for the mission God gave him."

"From the sound of things, she is from good Christian stock. I trust our son to be selective in choosin' a bride equal to him. Her brother, Clarence, David's roommate, has asked David to partner with him in plantin' a church in Marion. However, David's heart is set on ministerin' to the Chinese here in California."

Mary held the letter on her lap and closed her eyes. "Thank you, Lord, for watchin' over our children and establishin' their steps. Please bring clarity of your plans here in Snelling to David and especially to his fiancé. Relocatin' will be a grand step for her to take far from her family. Also, she will be newly wedded and ministerin' to unfamiliar people. Lord, help her."

"Amen," Jonathan said, leaning back in his chair and scratching at his beard. "The weddin' will occur durin' harvest, which may pose some difficulty with the new farm."

"No, Jonny. You wouldn't miss your son's special day?"

"I'd rather not. I trust my employees at Sower Farm to operate without any hiccups. However, I'm afraid Samuel will have to stay behind to keep a watchful eye on the superintendents at S&S Farm."

Mary pouted. "Yes, I must agree with your assessment, dear."

A walnut-size stone seemed to form in Naomi's throat and fall to her stomach as she listened to her parent's volley over another upcoming family milestone. Her eyes began to sting.

David beat me to the altar. I'm the only one left of my siblings who hasn't found a spouse. I'll never find me a husband in this small town. I'm goin' to become an old maid livin' on my father's farm, milkin' my father's cows for the rest of my life. Confusion circled her entire frame — a husband. Sarah and Samuel found their forever partner here in Snelling. Why can't I? Am I destined to be a spinster? Oh, dear Lord, I pray not!

"Oh, phooey!" Naomi stomped and clenched her fists. She should be expressing gladness for her brother's good news, but no words would come to her mind. Frustrated, she ran upstairs to her bedroom and tumbled into her bed. Planting her tear-streaked face on her pillow moistened its hand embroidery.

The sound of footsteps followed up the staircase and into her room. A warm body sat on her bed's edge, and a gentle hand rested on her back. "Naomi, dear, don't cry," her mother's compassionate voice intensified her sorrow.

How could she possibly know what I'm thinking?

"Oh, Mama. I'm such an ugly ducklin', and I'm afraid I'll never marry. You and Pa may be stuck with me. I'm sorry to disappoint you, but I may never be as established as you've hoped."

"My darlin' daughter, your time will come. You and that special gentleman just haven't crossed paths yet."

"How will I ever cross any man's path in this small town? I'm more likely to cross a turkey on the road, than a man that would love the likes of me."

"Don't you lose heart, my daughter. Sir Thomas Overbury said in his poem, 'And all the carnal beauty of my wife, is but skin-deep,' and furthermore, 'God's image in her soul, o let me place my love upon! Not Adams in her face.'

"A woman's true beauty is her virtue, which you are greatly endowed, Naomi. A faithful and loving wife is more precious to a man than her physical beauty."

Naomi could not control her tears. Oh, so you agree with me, Ma? I lack facial allurement and graceful attributes. I know you mean well, Ma, but that statement is not helping me at all. Sobs poured like rolling rain and thunder.

Mary continued to encourage her daughter. "You keep prayin' and knockin' on the Lord's door. Make your request known as the widow did with the unjust judge in the parable Jesus spoke about in Luke 18. Now, if the unjust judge harkened to her cries, Jesus tells us, God, who is a righteous and loving judge, will all the more respond to the cries of His people. So, He will hear you too, darlin'.

"Keep remindin' God of your ideal husband. Believe me. He is out there and will be a reflection of you, and you his. God tells us it's not good for a man to be alone, and so He fashioned Adam's wife from his own body, his rib. You'll be an excellent helpmate and will one day make your husband proud."

Naomi allowed her mother's words to bring comfort. The scripture she shared made sense to her and gave her hope. The Lord cannot ignore her forever. He will have to heed her annoyance. Begrudged, she propped herself up and lay her head on her mother's shoulder. "Thank you, Ma. I needed your encouragement."

"You must cling to the Lord's promises in His word." Her mother squeezed her close. "All right, dear. Let's be happy for your brother. He'll want you there for his weddin'. You two are very close to one another, and he misses you somethin' terrible. Not only will he ask for me and your pa's acceptance of his bride, but he'll also want yours as well. He'll be pleased if his wife and best sister got along well with one another like you and Jia-Li are best of friends. Aren't you in the least curious who your brother fell in love with?"

"Yes. Of course, I am. Knowin' my brother, she has met all the virtuous wife criteria in Proverbs 31:10-31." After wiping the tears from her eyes, she tugged at her blouse and skirt's wrinkles. "I'm done feelin' sorry for myself. Let's go downstairs and start preparin' for the next Sower weddin'. Whew…two in one year." She kissed her mother's cheek.

"Good. That's my girl."

7

Durum and Darnel

Opening the window shutters, Jonathan allowed the California sunshine to warm his face and the farmhouse office. June and the green acres of wheat at Sower Farm grew to full height with budding heads. The gentle breeze moved the knee-high stalks like the rolling water on Merced Falls River. The farmhand's muffled chatter and the horse's neighing waft in the temperate arid air in a melodious fashion to douse pleasure in Jonathan's ears. Although his body ached and his bones creaked from the physical toll the farm took upon his life, Jonathan never tired of watching and participating in the day to day activities at his beloved homestead.

The Sower Farm supervisors, Yung, Sheng-Li, and Anguo, were saddling their horses in the corral to make their daily inspection of the grounds. Lad approached the farmhouse on horseback, waved to the staff, and met Samuel, who waited for him on his horse, Fire. The smiles on their faces and cheerful greeting indicated a positive change in their attitude as they rode down the wayside path headed to S&S Farm. The heavy blanket of dread seemed to lift from his apprehensive son and son-in-law.

I'm so glad my boys are muddlin' through together just fine. They make a perfect team. Lord knows they need to be watchin' each other's backs around the new superintendents at S&S Farm. It seems they've adjusted to their new responsibilities. At the dinner table, when they return home at the end of the day, they're mentionin' fewer complaints and only a couple of minor incidents. Despite their lack of adequate farmin' equipment and laborers, they must be makin' good progress. They do seem more pleasant these days.

"Mr. Jonathan, here is your coffee," Jia-Li said as she entered the office and carried a tray to his desk. A small mound press up against her calico maternity day dress.

"Ah, thank you, darlin'. How are you feelin' today? Is your stomach still ailin' you? Are you able to keep your meals in your belly?" Jonathan said, walking to her and pouring himself a cup.

"A little better. Gracious of you to ask. Mother has been preparing ginger tea for me, and it helps. We've decided, for now, I wash dishes and clean kitchen while she cooks. The smell of stir fry makes me ill." She rubbed her belly. "I do crave Mrs. Mary's pickled cucumbers and salted eggs."

"That's a fine arrangement. Do what you must. You women know what is best when it comes to bein' with child. Please don't overwork yourself now, and be sure to eat and drink plenty of fluids when you are able. I want my grandchild to be strong and healthy too." Her father-in-law smiled, winked, and sat down at his desk with his coffee.

"Oh, Mr. Jonathan, not to worry. I take good care of baby. Me and Samuel so very happy." Her entire being glowed. "May I get you anything else?"

"No, dear. I'm so delighted too." He plunged into his paperwork as Jia-Li exited the room.

A few minutes after the grandfather clock chimed ten times in the foyer, a knock came at the front door, greeted by the butler, Jia-Li's father.

"Ah Huang-Fu, I need to speak to Mr. Jonathan," said the familiar voice.

"Sure, sure. Come in. Sit down in parlor, and I will tell him you are here," Huang-Fu said. A soft tap on Jonathan's office door and the butler entered.

"Pardon me, sir. Ah Yung wishes a moment with you."

"Please let him in, Huang-Fu."

The lead superintendent trudged into the office with a fist full of wheat stalks and held them before his employer.

"What do you have there, Yung?"

"Mr. Sower, please examine and tell me what you see."

Jonathan adjusted his spectacles, reached for the samples, and brought them closer to his face. An immediate recollection came into view, and the feeling of dismay whirled inside him. The wheat grains grew in two even rows on the stalk, like an ear of corn, whereas the darnel heads clustered in groups on the shoot.

"Tares. Are there vetches growing in our wheat?"

"I am sorry to tell you, but yes, Mr. Sower."

"How much?"

"Maybe about ten percent of crop. Would you like we pull them out?"

Jonathan's mind imagined the farmhands yanking out the harvest as they removed the invading grass. "No. Let's not do that unless we remove the wheat too. Just let them grow with the good grain. Then at harvest time, instruct the men to separate the durum from the darnel. We will burn the weeds afterward."

Jonathan scratched at his beard. "How in the world did the tare seeds get mixed into our wheat seed? The flour mill wouldn't do such a thing. And last year's crop did not produce any tares. Hum, this baffles me."

"I do not know, sir." Yung gripped his fist behind his back and paced by the window as he viewed the barn in the distance. "The burlap bags containing the grain were sealed when we pulled them from the barn. Nothing has changed in our procedures. I observe the men opening the bags and placing the seed in the wooden crates before being sown the next week. If any tampering occurred, it would take place that weekend before we planted the seeds in the fields." He stopped, brows furrowed and eyes locked on Jonathan. "Pardon me for asking, but are you aware of having any enemies that would sabotage your industry?"

"Well, I have my competitors, but they wouldn't stoop to a dastardly deed such as this." Jonathan joined Yung at the window and ran faces through his mind. He recalled the recent squabble on his second farm. "Come to think about it, Harold and his boys at S&S Farm might be the possible suspects. They weren't excited about training with you men. Besides our staff, they are the only ones who are aware of our timing procedures to sow seeds. All other farms in our area were still plowing their fields when we were ready to plant."

Anger stewed in the wheat baron's belly. He slammed his right fist into his left palm several times and returned to his desk. "Those S&S superintendents are the only ones stupid enough to consider this tomfoolery. They expressed their unhappiness about me takin' over Maxfield's business. I have a stinkin' suspicion they are behind all the mishaps with Samuel and Lad. They think they are a clever bunch and can outsmart us. Sin will always rear up its ugly head. They are bound to slip, and we will find evidence of their folly. Everyone must keep a sharp eye so that we can prove their guilt."

Ah Yung stood in front of Jonathan's desk, anticipating further instruction. "Yes, sir. I will inform my men to be watchful and be doubly sure to secure the barn when they leave at the end of the day."

"It's a fine mess, we've got on our hands." Jonathan sat and leaned back in his chair, rubbed his temples, and then focused on his lead superintendent. "Well, Yung, do your best to find out where the tare came from. I'll inform Samuel and Lad of this situation and urge them to comb their farm for any evidence."

Waving his arms around him, Jonathan pointed to the barn and the fields. "Check everywhere and everything, but be discrete. If the culprits are amongst us, you won't want to scare them away. We'll want to witness these bad boys doing their dirty work and arrest them. They can't get away with this mischief."

"Yes, sir. I will do my best, although I do not suspect any of our staff. I will search for evidence, but it happened almost four months ago. If any mischief should happen, it will occur when the S&S men return in the fall when they come to train on the harvester."

"Hopefully, we can resolve this mystery by July. I plan to have a staff luncheon here at Sower Farm before my family and I leave for Indiana to attend my youngest son's wedding in August. We may be away for almost a full month. Samuel will stay behind to manage both farms. However, I'll need all employees workin' in unison under his directive.

"I will investigate immediately and report any findings before next luncheon." Yung bowed and excused himself.

Jonathan examined the durum and darnel samples in front of

him and imagined the infestation growing amongst his prize crop. The work to separate the weeds from the wheat will add time to the strict harvesting schedule. However, he is still far ahead of his competitors. Getting to market will be close with the added delay, but he can still achieve his goal.

Infuriated, Jonathan closed his eyes and prayed to calm himself. Dear Lord, please reveal to me my enemies and give me wisdom and strength to confront them and put an end to these shenanigans.

8

Count the Cost

"Thank you once again for the delicious home-cooked meals and splendid weekend." David grinned, wiping his face with the cloth napkin as he leaned back in the wood slat chair and addressed the Harrington family and his fiancé sitting beside him. The distant whistle of the five o'clock train blew as it rolled into town ready to take passengers back to Upland, where the lonely campus dormitory awaited David and other students who remained during summer break.

"You're always welcome, dear," Catherine said as she and her daughters started clearing the table. "I'm sure your mother is quite the cook herself living on a ranch such as theirs."

"She sure is, or was, before we acquired our Chinese domestic help. Now they do most of the cooking for the family."

"Oh, and what type of meals might they prepare?"

"Both American and Asian entrees." David closed his eyes and licked his lips as he recalled the savory dishes. "I sure do miss their cuisine too. Can't wait to get back home," he said, daydreaming with a satisfied smile settling on his face. The sound of silverware splashing in the dish tub and quick steps crossing the dining room disrupted his thoughts. Eyes wide open, he saw the backside of Clara in her green and yellow plaid tea gown swishing out the front door to the porch.

David glanced at the bewildered faces in the room. Their raised brows expressed his puzzled thoughts regarding Clara's sudden dismissal. "Is Clara all right?"

"I'm not sure, David. She seems snippy of late," Catherine said.

"Must be from the wedding plan pressures coming up next month. Uncle Hampton has made it clear that he will make all arrangements and provide the funds for a grand celebration worthy of his family. His highly esteemed reputation is at stake." Cora grimaced as she put the dirty dishes in the basin.

"What exactly do his plans entail? Clara and I want only a simple country wedding."

Catherine gagged. "I'm sorry, David. I tried my best to argue your case, but the best attorney Marion has to offer is quite difficult to challenge. Besides, he is not only my eldest brother, but he is also the only surviving relative on both sides of our family. If he and Aunt Alice had children of their own, I'm sure matters would be different. My children are his only heirs and recipients to their excessive abundance."

David clenched his jaws to withdraw unspeakable anger welling up inside him then pound his fist on the table. "I'll go see what's troublin' her." He pushed his chair aside to follow after Clara but did not find her on the front porch. David could scarce recognize her gentle voice streaming from the home's side garden.

Who is she talking to? Bending his ear toward her voice, he recognized the familiar one-way exchange. No…she's praying. He paused not to interrupt her and chastised himself for eavesdropping.

"Lord, please give me the strength and courage to be a proper pastor's wife. It's one thing to minister to my kind, but to serve the Chinese is asking a lot from a simple country girl. I'm afraid, Lord. California might as well be China. Both places are foreign and frightening to me." Clara's words trembled.

"Lord, forgive me if I sound like an ungrateful child. On the contrary, I thank You so much for finding the perfect husband for me. No Christian woman can ask for any better. I'm so in love with him."

David stopped breathing in anticipation of her saying the dreaded conjunction.

"But Lord … I don't think I can marry him. I'd be leaving my family, my home, to live with strangers and a territory I know nothing about." She said it. Frustrated whimpers followed.

Shocked by her concealment, David began his prayer as he gripped the porch rail. "Father, forgive me if I've been too hasty. My love for Clara consumes me. Marriage seems to be the solution I need to propel me forward to preach and teach the gospel. I hoped Your plan for me included her. I can't imagine ministering without her by my side to encourage me. Oh Lord, maybe I should take up farmin' like the Sower men before me and find some property here in Indiana so she can be near her folks."

The Holy Spirit in him tugged hard at his heart from the grievous thought, which caused David's mind to race and reason. "Perhaps I'm wrong, and she isn't ready for marriage, and we aren't equally yoked with the same vision. Father, if she is to be mine, then please calm her fears and open her eyes to share the gospel with the Chinese." Pausing for the Lord's response, the Holy Spirit quickened him with Luke 14:26-35.

'If any man come to me and hate not his father, and mother, and wife, and children, and brethren, and sisters, yea, and his own life also, he cannot be my disciple. And whosoever doth not bear his cross and come after me, cannot be my disciple. For which of you, intending to build a tower, sitteth not down first, and counteth the cost, whether he have sufficient to finish it? Lest haply, after he hath laid the foundation, and is not able to finish it, all that behold it begin to mock him, saying, "This man began to build, and was not able to finish." Or what king, going to make war against another king, sitteth not down first, and consulteth whether he be able with ten thousand to meet him that cometh against him with twenty thousand? Or else, while the other is yet a great way off, he sendeth an ambassage, and desireth conditions of peace. So likewise, whosoever he be of you that forsaketh not all that he hath, he cannot be my disciple.

Salt is good: but if the salt have lost his savour, wherewith shall it be seasoned? It is neither fit for the land nor yet for the dunghill, but men cast it out. He that hath ears to hear let him hear.

Sweat beaded on David's forehead and palms. His heart pounded hard and forced his lungs to gasp for air. He loosened the bow around his neck and tried his best to suppress the agony he felt knowing he must sacrifice his love for Clara for the sake of following after his calling. In distress, he ran to the adjacent cornfield and hid so others would not observe him as he cried out to God.

"Lord! How can you ask this of me after all we've been through together? You know my heart and how much I love you. I thank you for being my best friend and being there for me when no one else seemed to care. Yet you test me?" He fell to his knees and pound the dirt. "Did you not provide a helpmate for Adam? Then why not for me?"

His thoughts moved to his family, and an angry chuckle passed his lips. "Father, the irony baffles me. You've placed me in a large household endowed with abundant blessings, yet I'm the loneliest of souls, forgotten and tossed to the wayside. Am I to be alone to fend for myself the rest of my life?"

David wept as he brought his knees to his chest, wrapped his arms around his legs, and peered upward at the first star shining in the dusk sky. "If Your desire is for me to serve You in celibacy, then …" his heart fell into the pit of his stomach, displacing the deepest despair "… I shall abstain from requesting a wife and count the cost. I will break my engagement with Clara and see her no more. I'll place all my focus on completing my studies and return to California to complete the task You started through me. I'll nail my selfish needs to the cross to die so that I might be Your disciple." A picture of Jesus dying on the cross appeared in his mind's eye.

Jesus sacrificed Himself for the sake of fulfilling the mission His Father placed in His life to take the punishment of other's sins so they may be saved from spiritual death and receive eternal life in heaven.

For the first time, David experienced a vicarious understanding of Jesus's sacrifice. He now shared in the suffering for the gospel as the apostles once did. A comradery with Christ, he fully understood through his situation. He realized the magnitude of Jesus' forfeiture as He gave up His kingdom, His relationship with His Father, His earthly family, and friends, to have a family of His own, and even give His life to complete the mission to save lives.

Truth gripped David's conscience, and his sacrifices did not compare. Jesus is God, the King of the universe, and He surrendered much.

I am a farmer's son, but Jesus must've found something worthy in me to die for. Of course, He did. He came as a humble carpenter's son and understood the meek's humility. Psalm 51:17 tells me that the sacrifices of God are a broken spirit: a broken and a contrite heart, O God, thou wilt not despise.

"Oh, Lord. I am so sorry for my selfishness and frailties, for I'm not strong like You. Forgive me. My needs are nothing compared to what You gave up for me. Who am I to be making these demands? I am Yours since You paid the price for me with Your death. Do with me as You please. I trust You and am aware that You desire the best for me. You understand me better than myself, and if You think I can complete this mission on my own, then I shall obey. I believe You will always be with me, so I will never be alone. I thank You, Lord, for orchestrating my life." David breathed deep. "I know what I must do."

David picked himself off the ground and shook the dust from his clothes. As he turned toward the house, there stood Clara between the cornrows, her emerald eyes doused in tears.

She rushed into his embrace. "Oh, my love, you will not be alone. Your helpmate is here and ready to trust in the Lord. He spoke to me too. He gave me Joshua 1:9 to cling to. Be strong and of a good courage; be not afraid, neither be thou dismayed: for the LORD thy God is with thee whithersoever thou goest."

9

Out of the Heart

Jonathan and his son, Samuel, ensconced themselves at each end of the long table set for sixteen staff members positioned under the expansive oak tree's shade beside the Sower farmhouse. Naomi, Sarah, Lad, Harold, Leonard, Grier, and Nevil sat to Jonathan's left. Mary, Liang, Huang-Fu, Yung, Sheng-Li, Anguo, and Jia-Li to his right. The spit cooked luncheon would be served by temporary hired help for that day, so the permanent employees may enjoy the respite from their duties and focus on his announcements.

The tension emanating from the four Sower and Sons Farm superintendents rose as thick as bread dough leavened by evil. Harold, Leonard, Grier, and Nevil glared at the Chinese staff who sat across from them who kept their heads low and focused on the western utensils and cuisine of steak, potatoes, and vegetables set before them.

How in the world will I be able to leave this place with a good conscience knowing the hatred which lurks in the heart of the new superintendents? Lord, You give me no choice but to trust in Your mighty hand to keep matters under control while we are gone. Jonathan stood, searched the stern faces staring back at him, bowed his head, and said grace. "Dear merciful Father, I thank You for the fine group of men and women here at this table who are under my employ.

I ask for Your blessings upon each of them and the fruit of their labor. Bless this meal we are about to receive and the day ahead of us. In Jesus' name. Amen."

Napkins fell on laps, and silverware clattered as the group on his left devoured their fare. Except for his wife, those on the right responded much slower.

Soft-spoken Mandarin passed between the Suens and the Sower Farm superintendents as they fumbled with their forks and knives. After cutting their steak and potato into small and more manageable pieces, their food appeared more like the stir-fried cuisine they prepare daily. Jonathan realized his temporary help failed to provide chopsticks for his culturally diverse staff. Uncommon to his white employees, yet very normal to his Chinese team, they wiped their hands on their napkins and began consuming their meal with their fingers.

The S&S superintendents' focus did not leave the SF workforce. Their jaws dropped disturbed by the unusual sight.

"Criminy," Leonard said. "They're eating with their dirty hands."

"Savages!" Nevil jeered and hurled spit on the ground.

Grier nodded, huffed, and wiped his mouth on his sleeve.

"Disgustin'." Harold put his utensils down and sent a sharp glance at Jonathan. "You expect us to share the same table with these sticks?"

The back of Jonathan's neck tingled as his blood boiled. Suppressing his anger, he waved to one of the waiters who hustled to his side. "Would you please go to the kitchen and fetch seven sets of chopsticks for me and some of our staff?"

"Make that eight," Mary said.

"No nine!" Samuel guffawed.

Naomi, Sarah, and Lad exchanged whispers and nods between themselves.

"Why don't you make that twelve," Lad grinned from ear to ear. Without hesitation, the waiter executed the command and rushed inside the farmhouse.

Not skipping a beat with his family's keen perception, Jonathan put his fork down and scooped a handful of vegetables and brought it to his mouth. After chewing and swallowing his food, he turned his focus on Harold. "If you want to continue to be a Sower and Sons employee, then you'll need to get used to eating with us 'sticks'."

Jonathan snickered. "Let me make it clear to you as Jesus once said, 'Whatsoever entereth in at the mouth goeth into the belly, and is cast out into the draught? But those things which proceed out of the mouth come forth from the heart, and they defile the man. For out of the heart proceed evil thoughts, murders, adulteries, fornications, thefts, false witness, blasphemies: These are the things which defile a man: but to eat with unwashen hands defileth not a man.'"

The four S&S men lowered their eyes and said nothing more.

"Who needs chopsticks?" The waiter asked and distributed the utensils to the raised hands. Chuckles and small talk passed among the Sowers, Suens, and the SF superintendents as they consumed their meal with the Asian utensils and their hands.

Once everyone finished eating, Jonathan made his announcements as he paced behind his seat. "I've called this luncheon, not only to show you my appreciation for the hard work all of you have done so far at both farms during this transitional period but also to inform you about an event which will take place in August.

"I'm still optimistic in our progress, and the goal we are going to achieve together despite the few minor incidents which occurred at farm two, and the tares found in our crop at farm one." Jonathan paused and locked eyes with each employee for a few seconds and more so with the S&S superintendents who did not flinch a muscle and kept their poker faces. However, Harold's Adam's apple slid down his reddened neck as if he swallowed a large lump of guilt.

"Next month will put your skills to the test. My youngest son, David, will be getting married in August, and my entire family will be attending his weddin' in Indiana except for Samuel and Jia-Li, who will stay behind and manage both farms until we return." Jonathan peered at his eldest son, who sat tall, chin up, having a confident air about him.

"Business will continue as usual, although your duties will increase. Samuel will be overseeing my responsibilities in my office. I expect each of you to report to him. I have instructed him to send experienced Sower Farm workers every week to Sower and Sons Farm to assist with the new equipment operations and maintain a timely schedule." Again he glanced at the S&S superintendents. This time Nevil's eyes bulged, and

Grier's jaw muscles clenched.

"Inspections will take place when I return ... whenever that will happen. We will try to be back for the harvest. I'm not sure of the precise time, but I give you my word. Be watchful and on top of your tasks, and you will always be prepared for me. Any questions or comments?"

Yung raised his hand.

"Yes, Superintendent Yung."

"Mr. Sower, I hope you don't mind me asking. Will you be providing special bonus at end of harvest if our work pleases you like you did last year when you went to Columbia?" Yung's eyes sparkled, and an eager grin covered his face.

"Good question indeed, Yung." Jonathan crossed his arms and paced a few steps as he contemplated his current financial situation. "Well ... it all depends. If we can recover from our losses from the tares at farm one and if the farm two superintendents can bring the wheat to market early so that the flour mill offers the best price for our produce, then yes, you all can expect an added monetary bonus for your hard work."

Glistening grins and handshakes exchanged amongst the SF employees as grunts and smiles of uncertainty escaped the S&S superintendent's lips.

"Is there a problem, Superintendent Harold?"

"Uh, oh no, sir. You can count on us." The lead S&S superintendent hacked like a cat coughing up a hairball.

"All right. That is what I expect from both teams." Jonathan scanned the faces of all his staff. "This meeting is adjourned. Enjoy the remains of this day."

HUANG-FU'S INSTINCTS prompted him to assist the temporary help as they cleared the table. While grabbing his napkin, his fork fell to the ground. Pushing his chair aside, Huang-Fu stooped down on his hands and knees to retrieve the utensil from under the table.

"Ah...there you are." The fork had fallen near the lead S&S superintendent's boot. When reaching for it, the engraved artwork on Harold's heel bands drew the butler's eyes. Snakes. An intense shiver ran down Huang-Fu's spine as the remembrance struck a nerve. Then he overheard the S&S superintendents whispering amongst themselves.

"Hey Harold, we're not goin' to let them Coolies beat us to market, are we?" Leonard sneered.

Coolies … his laugh! The flood of painful memories began to come back.

"Of course not. We must learn how to use this new farmin' equipment fast. Only wished we used this method when we worked for Maxfield," Harold said and grunted.

Maxfield … his scratchy voice. These are the men who attacked me on Merced Falls Road! The sudden recognition frightened Huang-Fu, made him jump, and bump his head under the table.

Before he could scoot out from underneath, Grier bent down and peered below. "What do we have here?"

Those evil, angry eyes! The startled butler remembered the thug's glower as he stood before him, holding the driftwood used to pulverize his body.

Fear pulse through Huang-Fu's veins, which cause him to shiver beyond his control. "I, I drop fork," he said as he hastened out from under the table and squirreled himself behind his employer.

How am I going to tell Mr. Jonathan? He must be made aware of these evil men, but he also needs them right now. Should I tell him before he departs for Indiana or wait till he returns? He and his family need this time away from the farm. I do not recall a time when they have ever taken a holiday from this place. This news would cause him stress when rest is what he seeks. Heart and mind debating one another, Huang-Fu resumed busking the table after the disgruntled S&S men scurried away to the corral to fetch their horses.

"This may be the evidence that Mr. Jonathan has been searching for to bring these men to justice," he mumbled to himself in Mandarin. His heart swelled with relief as his conscience retaliated with thoughts of the Sowers with sour countenances caused by his appalling news.

No! I must wait until they return. Why destroy their well-deserved respite? Painful images of his attack loosed itself from a forgotten closet in his mind, and his emotions volleyed. What if something terrible happens while they are away? I can prevent it from happening if I notify Mr. Jonathan so that he can prepare beforehand?

Huang-Fu grappled with himself and concluded. Ó, tiān nǎ, wǒ bùnéng. I cannot ruin their holiday. Then an idea flashed through his mind as clear as day—calm and resolute subdued his fears. I shall inform Mr. Samuel instead. He will decide what is best for his family.

10

Farmhands Sent

Samuel squeezed Jia-Li's shoulder as they stood on the front porch watching his family's carriage depart Sower Farms headed to the train station in town. His thoughts returned to the previous year when he returned home after barely surviving on his own in California's unstable and fast-growing economy. Whew, I've come a long way in a short period. Now here I am married, soon to be a parent, and about to operate my father's enterprise on my own.

The planting season's busyness and the new farm equipment training kept the S&S superintendents occupied and, coincidentally, farm two incident-free the last few months. This moment of solitude worried Samuel about a possible underlying and uncontrollable rebellion while his father was away. Lord, help me!

"My love, do not worry. You will do fine." Jia-Li's steady and assuring voice brought him back to reality.

He turned to meet her glowing angelic face and realized God had already answered his life's call. Embracing her, he exercised caution around her growing abdomen.

"Where would I be without your love, understanding, and encouragement? You know my thoughts before I speak them. I am a blessed man."

A fluttering like wings came between them as he embraced her. Jia-Li giggled, and her eyes sparkled. "Ah … did you feel that?"

"I did!" Samuel placed his hand just below her stomach, and the gentle rolling movement repeated.

"And I am a blessed woman!"

HOW STRANGE TO BE SITTING BEHIND PA'S DESK. Samuel chuckled as he settled into the leather chair molded to his father's frame through the years. *The last time I sat here, I was knee-high, and this chair seemed like an enormous throne. Now it fits me like a well-tailored suit.*

A tobacco tin on the desktop recalled more memories of gagging on his father's clay pipe and stumbling when he wore Jonathan's gigantic shoes. *Who am I foolin'? I can never fill pa's role. Daydreaming seems to be what I am best at accomplishing.*

A gentle rap at the office door interrupted Samuel's fancy. Huang-Fu peered inside. "Mr. Samuel … Yung, Sheng-Li, and Anguo here. Are you ready for them?"

Samuel cleared his throat and sat tall. "Yes. Please let them in." The three SF superintendents entered, bowed, and sat across from him.

The sweet tobacco aroma which permeated the room instilled a vision of God sitting on His throne with incense bowls around Him and the multitude of saints at His feet singing praise songs. A deep sense of respect and reverence for his father enveloped Samuel as he temporarily procured the Big Augur position before the faithful employees with nervous smiles. *They too, must think it odd to see me sitting here instead of Pa.*

"Men … all things are possible through Christ who strengthens me." Samuel forced a warm smile to provoke calm and assurance. "The next few weeks will no doubt be difficult. Especially workin' at farm two with the new superintendents and trainin' on equipment unfamiliar to them. Without a doubt, I know they resent us. These fellas are clever devils."

Frowns and furrowed brows swallowed the tanned faces.

"We must watch each other's backs. Let's send in two men at a time starting with your team Anguo since it is still early in the season, and the fieldwork requires less pressure than at harvest."

Anguo returned a slow nod.

"We'll work our way up the ladder with two men from your group, Sheng-Li, and last from Yung's group. By then, the harvest will be upon us, and the more experienced men will be needed. Be sure to report to me your progress or of any trouble."

"Yes, sir," the three said.

"We will send our strongest and best men." Yung stood and shook Samuel's hand, and they returned to their duties.

THE GOLDEN SUN HUNG LOW over the wheat fields while Samuel sipped tea on the front porch rocker pleased because up to this time, the week ended without incident. As usual, he watched as the superintendents and farmhands gathered by the barn, loaded themselves on the wagon, and returned to camp at the west end of Snelling.

Unlike the past four days, Anguo did not board. Instead, he waved goodbye to the group and walked over to meet Samuel on the porch.

"Is everything all right, Anguo?"

"I am not sure, Mr. Samuel. The two farmhands I sent to farm two did not return yet. I will wait for them a little while longer. If they do not show, I will go find them."

Samuel inhaled slow trying to calm his racing heart. "Yes, let's hope for the best. Please sit down and have some tea, and we'll wait together. I'll go with you should the need arise."

After several minutes passed, the neigh of two horses with a slow gait approached from the wayside path's opposite end. Their unhurried movement caught Samuel and Anguo's attention.

"That's them, sir."

"But, I only see one rider."

"No, there are two. But one is lying on horse's back."

Samuel and Anguo jumped to their feet and ran to the farmhands and their horses.

"Ah Jie! What happened?" Anguo assisted the farmhand sitting upright off his horse. He let out a painful grunt as he fell into Anguo's arms. Samuel grabbed the reins of the other horse carrying the unconscious worker whose head dripped with blood from open gashes.

"We were attacked by masked thugs as soon as we left farm two," Jie said. "Ah Tem hurt bad. They beat us with river wood."

"All right. Let me fetch the carriage. We need to get you both to Doc Cassidy's right away." Samuel ran into the barn, hitched his horse to the carriage, and returned. After loading the injured farmhands, they moved with haste to the doctor's clinic where Jie and Tem would receive care.

"Doc, again spare no expense to treat these men." Samuel shuffled about his farmworkers as they lay prone on cots in the clinics examining room. Jie groaned in pain, and Tem's shallow breathing indicated a chance of survival.

"Not to worry, Samuel. I'll have them stitched and feeling no pain. After a few days of recuperation from their bruises and wounds, they can return to light duty. Tem may need more time. Be thankful. Matters could be worse."

Samuel shook the physician's hand. "Thanks, doc." He turned to his superintendent. "Let me take you home, Anguo. It's not safe for you to walk alone."

The two men left the clinic, board the carriage and head toward the west end of town to the Chinese camp. Heads held high they scan the surroundings for any possible perpetrators as they pass through the small town which basked in the dusk's grey shroud. The one-story wood houses' candlelit windows framed the picturesque activity indoors as residence prepared their evening meals and merry about without a care in the world. The contrast to the injustice his workers endured at the end of their day baffled and upset him.

"Will you report to sheriff, Mr. Samuel?" Anguo asked as the carriage came to a stop at the camp.

"Yes. I will stop by the courthouse and notify the marshal and his deputies of this incident. I hope you have a restful weekend, Anguo, and I'll see you next week."

THE DARKENED UPSTAIRS WINDOWS of the Snelling Courthouse proclaimed the end of the day and workweek. The dim glow from barred windows below and muffled chatter never ceased as prisoners conversed with their captors. An armed lawman always stood guard twenty-four hours a day, seven days a week, the entire year in the belly of the four-room jailhouse. During regular hours the marshal, sheriff, and their deputies occupy a large room.

Samuel entered the building's side door and expected a reduced staff to remain for the evening. Two lawmen with six-point star badges above their coat pockets sat at their desks, cleaning their service pistols. One badge had Sheriff inscribed on it. The other badge labeled Deputy Sheriff.

"What can we do for you, sir?" the sheriff asked.

"How do you do? My name is Samuel, son of Jonathan Sower, owner of Sower Farms on La Grange Road and Sower and Sons Farm on Snelling Road. I need to report a brutal attack upon two of our farmworkers."

The sheriff put his pistol in his hip holster and leaned back into his chair in an alert position. "You came to the right place, Mr. Sower. I'm Sheriff Ryan, and the fellow over there is Deputy Sheriff Davis. Please take a seat son and explain the occurrence."

Samuel sat at the chair next to the officer's desk. "My family is away for my brother's weddin' in Indiana, and my father left me in charge of both farms until their return three weeks from now. Normal operations call for me to manage and supervise all staff at Sower and Sons Farm. Because of my father's absence, I must conduct business from Sower Farms and send two of our Chinese farmworkers to the other farm in my stead, which began this past Monday."

Samuel leaned forward, propped his elbows on his knees, and locked his focus on the sheriff's face. Soon Deputy Davis caught interest and stood nearby as if the mention of the Asian residence triggered disturbance.

"The week near passed without a hiccup, until today. The two farmworkers did not return to Sower Farm as scheduled. Instead, they returned almost an hour later, bloodied and beaten. One of them was unconscious from head injuries. Their attackers were masked and used river wood to assault my men."

The sheriff scribbled notes on a sheet of paper. "Did they say where this took place?"

"Yes, sir. About a quarter-mile south of the bridge on Snelling Road."

"Where are your workers now?"

"I brought them to Doctor Cassidy's clinic."

"All right, Mr. Sower, I'll send a deputy first thing tomorrow to get their statement and any other information that can help us find the perpetrators."

"Thank you, sheriff." They shook hands. Samuel returned home filled with frustration and anxiety as his mind raced in search of possible suspects. In his heart, he believed the tragedy is linked to the S&S superintendents. But how? They are bound to slip up. The evidence is what I need to prove their guilt.

11

More than I Can Bear

S amuel and Sheng-Li met outside the barn to forewarn Ti and Yow before they departed on their horses toward S&S Farm the following Monday morning. News of their co-worker's attacks spread fast amongst the Chinese camp and the small Snelling community. The chill of the morning air aggravated Samuel's veiled apprehension. Arms crossed in front of himself, he did his best to convey calm and confidence. "The assault on Jie and Tem can't be coincident. I do believe they were targeted, and my suspicions tell me that the attackers are connected with the farmworkers at S&S Farm. Whoever these men are, they covered their tracks and identities well. No evidence was found at the scene just like Huang-Fu's ambushers last year."

"We've done nothing to offend them." Sheng-Li shook his head in dismay.

"No. At least not from what we can see. To me, the culprits are motivated by their jealousy of you and your countrymen's proven ingenuity and economic prowess. These evil men's pride will be their downfall." Samuel said as he focused on the two farm laborers' consternation. "You men stay alert. Do what you must to defend yourselves should you encounter a situation as your comrades did before you."

"Always, Mr. Sower. We are accustomed to this hostility," Ti said.

"But we are no match against guns," Yow fidgeted.

"Yes, you are correct," Sheng-Li said grimacing. "Have you men been trained with any martial art fighting skills?"

"My father taught me some," Ti said.

"I am the same." Yow's hands trembled and jerked while holding the reins, causing the horse to move back a few steps. "Whoa. It's all right, boy," he said in Mandarin.

Sheng-Li grabbed the horses bit to pull him forward. "Well, you both may want to practice your skills this week just in case something happens." He turned to his employer. "I will also notify the other workers to do the same. Most of us are disciplined with some form of martial arts because of the hostile conditions we've encountered in our homeland and here in America. It is our only form of self-defense other than our farming tools."

"My prayer is for the safety of our workers, and I hope no harm will come to any of you." Samuel shook his head as the men huffed. "If I could afford to arm my workers with guns, I would. There lies the quandary for me and my father. We are farmers, not soldiers, providing tools for life, not weapons for death."

Tilting his head back, Samuel looked to the waking blue horizon. "Better yet, we have the greatest protection of all, and that is the mighty hand of our all-knowing God, and we hope to equip our staff with the knowledge of Him. We must trust the Lord for His ways are higher than ours even if it may require sacrifice on our part for a greater good."

The workers nod in agreement, then kicked their horse's side with their heels and scampered away into the dusty wayside path, which seemed to swallow them whole. They weren't expected to be seen until the end of the day when the same trail would spew them back, bearing decent news from Sower and Sons Farm.

A dull pain ached in Samuel's abdomen caused by the stress of the responsibility he bore the last few weeks and the troubles which occurred to those in his care. His hope, while his family were away, is to prove his worth by completing the tasks given to him by his father with the competence, accuracy and reliability expected of a seasoned wheat baron's son.

He trudged back to the farmhouse office deep in thought and

prayer. Dear Lord, please watch after these men and reveal to us our perpetrators. Give me the strength and wisdom to endure the next few weeks while overseeing both farms.

THE SECOND WEEK ENDED, and again the two workers returned battered and broken by perhaps the same masked men on Snelling Road outside of farm two. This time instead of driftwood as their weapons, the thugs used stones, which left Ti and Yow with fractured limbs and unable to work. Samuel brought them to Doctor Cassidy's clinic, and the following morning he reported the incident to the local authorities.

After Samuel concluded his report with the sheriff, a staunch well-dressed bank clerk immerged from the vault area and tapped Samuel's shoulder from where he sat.

"Excuse me, Mr. Sower, I overheard you mentioning that you manage Sower and Sons Farm on Snelling Road," the clerk said.

"Yes, I do. How does this concern you, mister?" Samuel stood to address the gentleman with a turned-up nose.

"I understand you are conducting business on Frederick Maxfield's land. Are you aware that he is about to forfeit his property to the bank?"

Shock spiraled in Samuel's body. "What? No mention has been made to either myself or my father."

"I've sent several letters to Mr. Maxfield requesting payment as he is entering his third month in the rears. We've received no reply nor payment. The bank can extend grace for so long. We do understand he is ill, but business is business."

"How much time do we have before he forecloses?"

"The contract allows three months, however, given the situation, there may be a possibility of extending the grace period. The length of time will be determined by the board."

"Thank you for the warning. If the bank can hold off on any further action, my father returns in a couple of weeks, and I will be sure to notify him. He may have a solution for this predicament."

"I'll see what I can do. Thank you for your time." The bank clerk returned to his desk by the vault, and Samuel head out the door. As he stood outside and placed his hat on his head, he glanced at the post office catty-corner from the courthouse. His mind urged him to send a telegraph to his father to inform him of the compiled situations. However, his heart held him back.

Not yet. Let the family enjoy the wedding. Don't bother them with bad news during David's joyous occasion. I can handle this. Prove to Pa that the strong Sower stock runs in my veins.

"I'll send four armed men next week," he said to himself, then marched across the courthouse lawn, not allowing his mind time to change his decision.

THE FOLLOWING MONDAY at sunrise, Samuel spoke to the four workers who sat on the buckboard, waiting for instruction. Their fear-stricken eyes and clenched jaws held back their revolt. "Be sure to stay together when you leave farm two. Arm yourselves with your staffs. Be watchful at all times, and keep your ears open. Someone is bound to slip up and say something." He slapped the horse's rear, and it moved down the path.

Day after day, Samuel waited for news from the four men. But nothing. Their report deemed the same as the other workers sent before them. The S&S superintendents and the white farmworkers were cooperative, kind, and treated them with unnatural respect worthy of suspicion. There were no incidents that warranted investigation.

SAMUEL TRIED TO RELAX into his father's chair late Friday afternoon as Yung reported the good news of the timely progress at both farms.

"The fields are seventy-five percent harvested and on schedule," Yung said with worry lines crossing his forehead.

"If something were to happen, Yung, it would happen today.

All we can do is wait."

"Yes, Mr. Samuel. But the sun will soon set, and the men have not yet returned."

"Let's wait until dark. If they aren't back by then, then we will round up some of the sheriff's men and look for them."

"Yes, sir."

AN HOUR LATER and the sun settled well below the horizon. The shadows melted into one, and the night reigned. Faces glowing from the lantern's light, Samuel, Yung, and Jia-Li stood staring at the wayside path from the front porch hoping for any movement.

"All right, Yung, let's go." Samuel flung his rifle over his shoulder as Yung grabbed the lantern.

Jia-Li tugged at Samuel's sleeve. "My love, please be careful."

"I will darlin'. Please try not to worry." Samuel embraced her, then pried himself away. He and Yung mounted their horses and forged into the darkness touched by the lantern's dim reflection.

THE SCENT OF FRESH-CUT WHEAT lingered in the warm night air as Samuel, Yung, Marshal Warner, and several deputies scoured Snelling Road in search of the four Sower Farms field hands. The broken remains of one of the workers straw hat scatter at the end of the bridge that crossed the Merced River.

"Look, Mr. Samuel. Over there!" Yung pointed, kicked his steed's side, and sped to the location to identify the article as Samuel followed on his horse. "I saw one of the men wearing this hat this morning."

Samuel dismounted and held the lantern near the ground. "These footprints tell me there was a scuffle here."

"Help me," a faint cry came from below.

Samuel and Yung hung the lantern over the bridge. The silhouette shape of four bodies lay crumpled on the edge of the river.

"Yung, go fetch the sheriff and his deputies while I go down there and help the men." Without hesitation, Samuel slid down the steep bank as Yung mounted his horse.

Placing the lantern on the shore, Samuel ran to the closest body lying halfway in the water. He turned him over and searched for a pulse beneath his soaked shirt. Nothing. Samuel shook him, but no response. Dead. "No!"

Samuel's heart sank to his stomach's pit as hot tears skewed his vision. Adrenaline pumped through his limbs, giving him the strength to lift the deceased body and place him on the bank.

The next victim bent like a rag doll over rocks and boulders splattered with blood, his face swollen and body broken. You're a heartbeat away from death's gate. Samuel removed his jacket and placed it under the worker's head.

A few feet away lay another man beside crimson-stained driftwood. A horrific cry escaped him as Samuel turned him on his back. "Thank God you are alive, Ah Ti. It's me, Samuel. Be still. Help is on the way."

Hands and legs strapped in a lasso, the last man groaned. The horrific sight stirred in Samuel images of his father-in-law, Huang-Fu, cocooned in the same fashion a year ago.

"Ah Li!" Samuel untied the bewildered man as the sound of several horses hooves pounded the bridge above him, announcing helps arrival. Lord, this is more than I can bear. I realize tomorrow is David's wedding, but I must send a telegraph to Pa about this tragedy first thing in the morning. He will want to know.

12

The Wedding

David and his entourage stood at attention in front of the altar when the "Wedding March" song announced the glorious entry for his bride. The floral scent coming from the baskets of white roses and lilies permeated the air in the small church. He glanced at his resplendent family standing in the first pew, craning their necks for the grand entrance. The celebration's fineries and details arranged and funded by Hudson Wilcox Esquire overwhelmed David. Lord, all I wanted was a simple country wedding. I hope this intervening relative will not become a thorn in me and Clara's side.

On many occasions, his fiancé cried when she explained her frustration over the heated debate between her mother and the demanding uncle in regards to their marriage. As the eldest brother and only surviving relative of Catherine Harrington, Hudson insisted his sister obey his wishes to maintain his reputation as one of Marion's highly acclaimed attorneys. He and his wife, Alice, bore no children of their own, so his nieces and nephew became recipients of their affluence. To maintain family peace, Clayton Harrington stayed silent as his wife and her brother played tug-of-war over the wedding plans. Despite her attempts, Catherine always ended in defeat.

The flower-filled church, the courts fine tailored suits and flowing gowns, the crowded pews overflowing with wealthy city dwellers, local farmers and family, all faded from view when the church's doors opened. Clara stood cloaked in white holding a bountiful bouquet as she clung to her father's arm. Delicate layers of satin and lace graced her slender bodice, and the warmth of her smile and her emerald eyes did not dim beneath the delicate veil covering her face. Clara's every step toward David made his heart swell. Now, here she stood exchanged from her father's hand to his. Soulmates for life. He wanted to shout for joy but maintained his composure before the pastor of the Harrington's church. The only decision allowed by her uncle.

Moderator Parr began. "Dearly beloved, we are gathered here today in the presence of Almighty God, to join in holy matrimony, Clara Harrington to David Sower…"

THE FOUNTAIN ROOM of Spencer Hotel bustled with wedding guests, where many of the out-of-town friends and family stayed during their visit, including the Sowers and the Hamptons. Hudson insisted the reception take place at the hotel where he practiced his profession in the structure's many leased offices behind the building.

Glistening silverware and fine china graced the linen-covered tables adorned with floral treatments and place cards. The bridal table stretched on one side of the room across the dance floor opposite the guests' tables. Garlands of white tulle and baby's breath arched from the ceilings chandeliers, and a large table at the entrance beckoned fanciful wrapped gifts from the invited. Sweet sounds resonate in the hall generated by the orchestra.

Cheers and applause escalate as the paired bridesmaids and groomsmen entered the room. The conductor announced, "Ladies and gentlemen, let me introduce to you, Mr. and Mrs. David Sower!" The crowd roared as the newlywed parade between tables, through the dance floor, and stood in court center in front of the bridal table.

The gaiety, hoopla, and laughter surrounded them like whirling snow in a blizzard. After a kiss before the guest, they walked over to the table closest to theirs reserved for immediate family. They hugged her kinfolk. But when David turned to do the same to his parents and siblings, they were nowhere in sight. Instead, the giant hand of Clara's uncle bolt toward his abdomen like a knife.

"Oh … Mr. Wilcox." A dead fish-like handshake is all David could offer Hudson. The lump in his throat staggered his speech. "I, I, I guess a thank you is in order for all you've done for our wedding day."

Hudson slapped David's back with a blow and wrapped his big arms around David's neck, almost as if a big brown bear took hold of him. "No problem, son. Anything to make my niece and her new husband happy."

Frustration and anger pushed David back. "Where are my parents and my family?" He said, doing his best to be cordial.

A wide grin crossed Hudson's face, proud of his accomplishments. "Oh…they are seated at yonder table." He pointed across the room.

David's eyes met his parents, Naomi, Sarah, Lad, and their children, who stood in blissful agony, applauding him and his bride. The stabbing pain in his heart reflected their embarrassment and shame for being snubbed by this annoying, narcissistic relative who took their seats. No, this won't do. This man will not replace my father and my family. That's enough. He turned to Clara, whose compassionate face understood the awkward situation. "Darlin', I need to take care of a matter. Would you mind if I pulled your uncle aside for a moment?"

"My husband, you do as you please." She smirked as if reading his thoughts. "Let's finish this day so we can start our own lives together."

David grabbed Hudson's elbow. "May I have a word with you in private … Uncle Hudson?" Before he answered, using a tight hold, David guided him to the hotel kitchen and laid into him.

"Mr. Wilcox … Uncle, Clara and I are grateful for your generosity. You far exceeded our desires for a simple country wedding. However, I need to address a flaw in your arrangements." Standing tall, he inhaled deeply. "As tradition holds, my parents and my siblings are to be seated at the table reserved for immediate family. I demand you trade seats with them."

Red-faced and shoulders sagged, Hudson stood dumb-founded. "I apologize. You're right. I will exchange seats with them immediately."

Eyes to his shoes, he shoved his fist in his pant pockets. "Go ahead now, and enjoy your wedding day."

"Thank you … Uncle." Firm grip, David shook his hand and returned to the reserved table to gather his bride as Hudson trailed behind him. "Come, Clara. Let's go greet my family."

At the table where the Sowers and Hamptons sat, David and Clara exchanged hugs and warm wishes, all the while surveying her uncle whisper in his wife's ear and discretely remove themselves from the reserved table.

"I believe the hotel staff misconstrued your seating arrangements." David grinned. "You are all to be seated at the table reserved for immediate family."

"We are just happy to be here to celebrate your special day," Jonathan said.

"Thank you," Clara said, "and we are so glad you came, father. We want you to be in every way a part of our celebration. Please sit with my parents, brother, and sister. Our families are one now."

The waiters combined both tables, and David's parents, siblings, nieces, and nephew soon joined Clara's. The best man lifted his glass and toasted the blushing bride and ecstatic groom. Roasted chicken or prime rib with a fresh garden salad and steamed vegetables tantalized everyone's palate, and the festivities began.

"Can I have all the bachelors come to the dance floor, please?" The conductor said as he pulled a chair in front of the bridal table. "Clara, please take a seat, and David kneel beside her." The eligible men crowded around the bride and groom. "Now David, this is only a preview of what's to come, so try to control yourself. Reach under your wife's gown and remove her garter."

Warmth rushed to David's face as he knelt before Clara and peered at her loveliness. *Am I to unwrap this beautiful gift before my guest?* His mind fast-forwarded to their honeymoon retreat at the newly built Kintner House Inn in Corydon a few hours away by train, made popular by those travelers practicing the bar when Hudson County court was in session. *Hudson amongst those people. Hum, is there a connection?* The thought of her uncle reeled in his wandering thoughts and back to the conductor's taunting.

"Hello? Do you need some help?"

White satin, lace. David focused on the hem of Clara's gown, then to her dainty shoes. Scripture from Songs of Solomon, The Beloved, came to his mind. How beautiful are thy feet with shoes, O prince's daughter! His body trembled as his gaze moved to her slender ankles.

"You'll have to lift her skirt to find the garter, young man." The conductor chuckled, and giggles rebound from the guest.

Hands shaking, David raised the hem and slid his hand up the curve of her left calf and the warmth of her silky thighs until his fingers touched the garter's gathered lace. Heat pushed beneath his shirt and pressure built, suppressed by his cravat. The joints of thy thighs are like jewels, the work of the hands of a cunning workman. The poetic scripture continued to flow in fragments. How fair and how pleasant art thou, O love, for delights! He didn't want to remove himself from the inviting garden. This thy stature is like to a palm tree … I said I will go up to the palm tree; I will take hold of the boughs thereof. Clara moved to his touch, which hastened him to complete his mission. David wrapped his fingers around the garter and slipped it down her leg as if carrying dates down the palm.

"You found it! Hip, hip, hurrah!" The conductor cheered as the audience roared with laughter. "Now gentlemen gather around. The fellow who catches this garter will be the next to wed. David, close your eyes, then slingshot the garter. Are you ready, men?" Like cattle running to water, the bachelors positioned themselves. The garter launched, the men lunged, and the victor rose to wave his prize.

"What is your name, young man? Please tell us a little about yourself," the conductor asked.

"My name is William Tyne," he said with a slight drawl, "I'm a good friend of the family. I own about 1500 acres of cornfield in Decatur County. I'm looking for a good wife to share my love and affections with and help me with business." His face scanned the audience and halted at David's sister, Naomi.

"All right. The rest of you men, please take your seats. Now let's have all the eligible ladies come forward. It's time for the bouquet toss."

THUMP, THUMP. Naomi's heart jumped at the opportunity, and so did her feet as she clamored to the dance floor with the others.

Clara stood, turned her back to the audience, and threw the bouquet over her shoulders. The floral bundle flew high and directly into Naomi's reach as if divinely guided.

Mouth agape, Naomi gasped for air, then pranced about like a filly which found its legs.

"And what is your name, young lady, and please tell us about yourself?"

"My name is Naomi Sower. I am David's sister and daughter of Jonathan and Mary Sower, who owns over 5,000 acres of wheat in California." She cast her gaze upon the audience and, as providence moved her, settled her sights upon William, whose attention fixated on her.

"Okay, folks, here they are. The next couple to be wed. Now let's begin with a waltz, shall we?" The conductor whisked away toward the orchestra, and the music began.

William hovered toward Naomi. "May I have this dance?"

His eyes. His smile. My Lord, I do believe I'm home. "Yes, you may." Placing her hand in his, they floated on the dance floor as if on a cloud.

THE UNUSUAL APPEARANCE of a courier talking to the bride and groom then rushing toward the reserved table caught Jonathan's attention and those sitting around him.

"I apologize for intruding on the celebration, but I have an urgent telegram for Mr. Jonathan Sower."

"Yes, over here, young man."

"I was informed you would be attending this wedding at the hotel." Embarrassed, the courier's face turned pinkish as he placed the note in Jonathan's hand. "Here you go, sir. Please sign here."

"Thank you." Jonathan signed and opened the envelope to read aloud its abbreviated content. He expected laudatory tidings from its sender since the telegraph arrived on his son's special day.

"Congratulations to David and Clara," Jonathan began with a smile and cheerful disposition. "Sorry," … this word alone clenched his heart and deflated his countenance, "bad news. Eight Sower farmworkers assaulted on Snelling Road. Seven injured, one dead. How should I proceed? Samuel."

13

The Heir

"Telegram for Mr. Samuel Sower," the courier said at Sower Farm's front door the following Monday.

"Yes. Very good. I will give to him."

Samuel detected the urgency in Huang-Fu's voice, hurried steps toward the office, and an intense rap on the door.

Huang-Fu didn't wait for permission to enter. "Telegram from Mr. Jonathan."

"Thank you." Samuel ripped open the envelope and read its content. "Pa wants me to investigate farm two. They boarded a train today and will be home in eight days. He asks that we do our best to handle matters." He inhaled and locked eyes with his father-in-law, who stood trembling across from him.

"Mr. Samuel ... I discover who attack me last year." Huang-Fu's face turned pale. "At staff lunch a month ago, I drop fork under table. When I went to pick it up, I notice snakes engraved on heel band of Mr. Harold's boots. It is same design on thug's boots who assault me!" Wagging his finger, Huang-Fu gasped, and his eyes enlarged. "I also recognize Mr. Leonard's voice and Mr. Grier's evil eyes."

Huang-Fu stumbled into a seat, his body shaking from the recollection. "I am so sorry I didn't say something sooner. I did not want to disrupt your family's plans to visit your brother on his special day."

Samuel bolt to his father-in-law's side to comfort him. Stupefied by Huang-Fu's declaration, he also felt gratified and relieved that his suspicions were correct and the culprits brought to light. This news is what he needed to put two and two together and to confirm the four S&S superintendents are behind all the horrible shenanigans. "No need to apologize. I understand because I too held back from informin' my parents of the recent incidents for the same reason."

Placing his hand on Huang-Fu's shoulder to calm him, Samuel's mind then race with the mishaps that occurred to him and Lad on farm two. I still need evidence indicating the S&S staff's involvement in the recent attacks and also the tares found at farm one.

"You must be very careful, Mr. Samuel. I am afraid for you."

"Don't worry. I will. There are no other options. This is the final week of harvest. The wheat will be ready to go to the mill next week. We can't afford to lose any more Sower Farm workers, so I must attend to it myself. Besides, I am the owner's son. What can they possibly do to me?"

Samuel stood and walked to the window overlooking the fields. "Lord, give me wisdom." Images of Jia-Li and their future children playing on the front porch clouded his mind as his father-in-law exited the room.

THE FAINT SOUND OF FARMHAND VOICES drifted into Frederick's bedroom window. The ailing land owner imagined the workers as they gathered bundles and placed them in wagons. The scent of fresh-cut wheat indicated the end of another promising harvest and the start to autumn's bountiful delights, which seemed to always relax him from the stressful demands of the planting season. Unlike years past, the reaper of the grand profitable prize will not be himself but rather his arch competitor, Jonathan Sower, from this point forward. The aggravating thought whirled about in his head, but he could do nothing about it with his health failing.

"One more bite, Mr. Maxfield," Nurse Agatha said as she shoved a spoonful of mashed potatoes in his mouth. A knock on the bedroom door disrupted their moment of solitude, and her head turned toward the unexpected sound. Distress crossed her brow, and she froze like a frightened deer. "Who might that be visiting you unannounced and entering your home without permission?" she said. "Surely, if it were an intruder, he would not knock."

Agatha placed the tray of food on the night table and wiped his mouth with a napkin. "Not to worry, Mr. Maxfield. I shall send him away." Heavy heels clicking on the wood floors, she charged toward the door expressing her troubled state of mind. Due to the financial strain Frederick's debilitating stroke condition caused, he had to dismiss his butler and cook several months earlier, which caused her added work. His medical care held utmost importance above all else, even at the expense of life's luxuries.

After opening the door, she slid behind it, hoping to prevent any unnecessary drama with the caller, which could upset her patient. Be that as it may, the thin wood frame doors did not prohibit sounds from entering into his room.

"I apologize, but I let myself in after waiting several minutes without an answer," said the familiar voice of his accountant, Augustus Durot. "I have an urgent matter to discuss with Mr. Maxfield."

"I'm sorry too, Mr. Durot, but you cannot just enter as you please unannounced in my employer's condition. You'll have to come back another day."

"No, ma'am. I must speak to him now unless you wish him to be out on the streets next week without a roof over his head and you without a job." Silence filled the air for a moment when the door opened, and both entered his room with caution.

"Mr. Maxfield, your accountant insists on seeing you," she said and allowed the persistent clerk to enter.

"Good afternoon, Fred," he said as he pulled a chair close to the ailing man's bedside.

"News?" Frederick forced a muffled sound from his half-paralyzed tongue.

The nurse scuffled about as if anticipating her employer's need for her assistance should the accountant's message generate a negative response.

"All is well on the farm," he said with a slight chortle. "The land is harvested, and the wagons are being filled to go to market next week. The men are quite ecstatic using the new harvester the Sowers provided. They are well ahead of schedule."

A bolt of jealousy ran through Frederick's veins, and he let out a rumbling puff from his lips. "Rent?" He gagged on some spit, knowing all too well the income source wasn't enough to cover his mortgage and his medical bills together.

"Yes, sir. The Sowers have paid their rent on time as usual. However, your medical bills continue to absorb most of your finances."

He unfurled a rolled note in his hand. "I hate to be the bearer of bad news, but I received this foreclosure letter from the bank today. Time has run out, but they are willing to extend you a couple more weeks because of your predicament. If they do not receive $500 by then, they will have to foreclose your property and claim the entire farm. I've exhausted every avenue you have and sold all liquid assets to make ends meet. Is there nowhere else you can locate these funds?"

Although anticipating the fallout of his dilemma, the alarming news still shook Frederick to his core, causing him to convulse. Without delay, Agatha came to his aide. *Five hundred dollars. Where am I going to get that?* He searched his thoughts, which brought recollections of drawing money from his safe to loan Leonard Lambert for his diabolical scheme to rid himself of an obscure Chinaman trespassing his yard. He paid him $450. With every shaking ounce of his being, he coughed out, "Leonard Lambert owes me."

THE FOUR S&S SUPERINTENDENTS and farmworkers were outside loading the last few acres of bundled wheat when Samuel arrived at farm two mid-morning the following Friday. The barn was empty as he had hoped to allow him time to investigate without their knowledge.

Samuel closed the barn door behind him and walked his horse to the furthest stall. "Wait here, Fire. I won't be long. We need to be out of here before the men come back for lunch." Not wasting time, he began combing the building, first downstairs between stalls, hay bales, feed barrels, and old farming equipment. Nothing. *These fellows are more intelligent than they appear. Perhaps I can find something upstairs.*

The slatted floorboards creaked as he meandered through the straw covering. Wheat seed sacks remained from the year's earlier planting season and stacked against one side of the loft. As Samuel inspected the area, a bundle of burlap with a different label painted in bright red stuffed behind the bags caught his eye. He grabbed them to read the bold print when four bloodied bandanas tumbled out. DARNEL SEEDS. Eight empty sacks and masks. His spine shivered at the connection. *At last, the evidence I need.*

As Sam shoved items into his long coat, the barn door opened that allowed sunlight to spill into the dusty building. *What? It's not even noon yet, and they're back.* Without hesitating, Samuel hid behind the wheat sacks to listen to the conversation and try to recognize the voices.

"Can't believe we're already done." The raspy voice and naiveté belonged to Leonard.

"Well, I do have to give Sower some credit. He did the right thing in using this modern harvesting equipment. Sure did save a lot of time and backache. We would've been ahead of the game if ol' boss Maxfield had done that too." The sentimentality could only come from the livestock superintendent, Nevil.

"It also helped not having those Coolies around and breathin' down our necks." The intimidated statement came from the lowest-ranked of them, Grier.

"Well, I don't think we'll be seein' the Sowers for a while. They'll be quite busy arrangin' funerals and visitin' the pill the next few weeks. You boys did a good job of fulfillin' Maxfield's wish to get rid of the foreign devils. Now we have to finish the ol' boss's request to kill the Sowers. That's the word he used when I last spoke to him about Jonathan pullin' out the wheat and plantin' fruit trees instead." That malevolent utterance befits no other than the senior of the group, Harold.

"I sure hope them Coolies won't live to remember what happened to them." Leonard guffawed like a donkey.

"At least one fellow won't be sayin' a word. I made sure his lungs filled with river water." A snarl rippled from Harold's laughter.

"How could they? I gave them a hard poundin' on their skulls with that driftwood." Grier snorted.

"If that didn't do it, then the stones would've done the job," Nevil grunted. "I believe Samuel is pretty shakin' up. Heck. He hasn't sent anyone all week."

"Now all we must do is take this wheat to the mill and pocket the money for ourselves. Who needs the Sowers? We can run this business without them. We'll need to be sure they don't step foot on this property again." An eerie cachinnation spilled from Harold's throat.

Leonard hooped and hollered. "That's the best idea yet, boss. Maxfield has his hound dogs on me to pay back the blood money he lent me to pay y'all for roughin' up the ol' Chinaman last year. He wants it by next week, or else he'll put me in jail for thievery." Stall doors opened, and wheels rumbled from the wagon used to fetch the farmworkers.

Stall doors. Oh no, Fire. Samuel's stomach turn to hear the evil confessions and plotting of the S&S superintendents and the thought of them discovering his horse.

"What do we have here? This isn't one of our geldings," Nevil said.

"Nope, you're right. That's Samuel's horse. It seems to me a spy is in the building," Harold said. "Where are you, Coolie lover?" He said aloud taunting. "Quick boys, find him and kill him. He heard everything we said. Heir or not, he's got to go."

Lord, help me. There is nowhere to run. Samuel's heart pound and perspiration drenched his shirt. Scuffling and the sound of crates toppling over resonate in the barn. The loft steps creak as the men climbed and went directly to where they hid all evidence of their evil deeds — the same location where he crouched like a sitting fowl awaiting its slaughter.

"There you are," Leonard said as he grabbed hold of Samuel's arm and Grier the other.

"You're a dead man, Mr. Sower," Nevil said.

Images of Jia-Li and his family flashed in his mind's eye as Samuel struggled from their grasp and met Harold's hate-filled gaze. "You may get rid of me, but know that you have sinned against the LORD: and be sure your sin will find you out." Moses' words from Numbers 32:23 flowed from Samuel's lips.

"Push him over the loft. Let's make it look like an accident, boys," Harold snarled.

"No!" Samuel buckled his knees, making it difficult for the men to carry him. Even so, his weight had no bearing on the evil flowing through the veins of these horrible men.

Up ... over ... down, down, down. Samuel landed hard on the crest of his neck. Pain shot through his skull, his back, his body. Soon darkness filled the room, and everything in sight disappeared.

14

A Good Sign

"I think I see their stagecoach coming around the corner, Fùqīn."
Jia-Li stood on her toes and shaded her swollen eyes from the
California sun's bright morning light as she and her father
awaited the arrival of her husband's family at Snelling's Wells Fargo
station. Small piles of dry oak leaves gathered by the late autumn winds
lay strewn about the road's edge and crunched beneath her skirt when she
moved with trepidation. A sudden kick to her ribs from her unborn child
conveyed its displeasure from its disturbed slumber. An instantaneous
response brought her hand upon her abdomen as if to quiet her baby.

"Nǚ'ér, please calm yourself. You must think of your baobao."
Huang-Fu's mirrored action caused him to wrap his arm around his
daughter's shoulder to steady her frantic emotions and the precious
bundle her body carried.

"How can I, father, when my husband is at death's doorstep?" Her
tears began to pool again. "His parents are not aware of what happened
to him. I am not sure how to tell them."

"You must speak the truth."

"But the truth is a lie. We know Sam did not fall from the loft by
accident. I believe the men who found him are the ones who pushed
him. The same men who attacked you." She whimpered then pulled an

embroidered handkerchief from her sleeve to dry her eyes. "Oh, Fùqīn, Samuel must live to tell us what really happened."

"Yes, daughter. All we can do is pray for a miracle."

HEAVY BREATHING DRAFT HORSES pulling the berry-red coach filled to maximum capacity clamored into town and completed their journey in front of the station. The doors flung open, and the passengers disembark with haste as the coachmen gathered their traveling bags. Searching the receiving crowd, Jonathan located his butler and daughter-in-law standing by the building's wooden walkway. As he and his family approached their momentary valets, he sensed an uneasiness about them by their lack of enthusiastic greetings.

"Hello, Huang-Fu … Jia-Li," he said, peering beyond them into the station anticipating his son's presence. "Where is Samuel?"

"Welcome home, everyone. We hope your time away bid pleasant and restful." Huang-Fu extended his reach to grab the carpet bags from his employer. "Mr. Jonathan, no time to waste. We must hurry to Dr. Cassidy's clinic."

"Wait a moment. Slow down. What do you mean? Have the injured men taken a turn for the worse?" The distressed wheat baron grasped his butler's arms. The last telegram he received about the tragic incident sent from Samuel a week ago engulfed him with immense melancholy and rage. Reason would explain his son's absence if he were attending to the disabled workers. Hoping for a definitive answer from his butler, he became distracted by his daughter-in-law as she wept and fidgeted behind her father.

Jia-Li stepped forward as the family diverted their attention to her enlarged abdomen beneath her shawl. Appalled expressions from passersby depicted the shameful indecency of a pregnant woman seen in public, all the more one of Asian descent.

"Samuel had a terrible accident at farm two. Mr. Harold thinks he slipped and fell from the loft last Friday. Dr. Cassidy said he fractured his skull and broke his back. He is in a coma and may not live,

Mr. Jonathan." Body trembling, her knees buckled, and she collapsed into her father-in-law's arms. A sudden hush came upon all the family members as they digested the unexpected, shocking report.

"No!" Mary shriek holding her hands to her lips as Naomi embraced her for support. Sarah and Lad gathered their family, shielding them from the horrific news.

"Wagon is across the street," Huang-Fu said with urgency in his voice.

"All right. Why don't you help the ladies and children board while Lad and I gather the luggage? Yes, let's go straight away to see Samuel." Disbelief gripped Jonathan's heart, yet in his mind, this tragic occurrence deemed deliberate considering the volatility at S&S Farm.

On the way to the clinic, Huang-Fu divulged the events of the past week leading up to Samuel's accident. He also included the discovery of his assailants, which occurred during the staff luncheon over a month ago.

The emotional extremes of happiness at David's wedding to the jarring news of Samuel's near-death condition stupefied Jonathan and his family. *My son's fall is not accidental because it would take a calculated move to jump the loft wall. No doubt someone assisted him.* The alarming situation sent bolts of pain through his shoulder, much like the near-fatal mini ball assailed him during the civil war. *Dear God, give me the strength to endure this battle.*

"SAM, ITS PA AND MA. We're back, son. Please wake up." Jonathan held Samuel's hand and stroked his almost lifeless face.

"Your son took a hard fall. It's a miracle he is still alive. He must have a strong will to live." Dr. Cassidy viewed the entire Sower household gathered around and rested his sight on Jia-Li.

"How long will he be like this doctor?" Jonathan asked.

"Difficult to say, if he recovers at all. Last Friday, I let out some blood from his skull to reduce the pressure. Let's hope he gains consciousness soon. Intravenous therapy alone will not keep him alive. He will need solid sustenance. And if or when he awakens, a strong possibility of amnesia and paralysis can occur. His spine is bruised and swollen. How severe is yet to be determined. All I can tell you is expect the worse, but pray for the best."

"When can we take him home?" Jia-Li asked as she held Samuel's other hand.

"It might be a while, dear. I will evaluate his condition after he wakes. Some form of physical therapy may be needed to strengthen his back so he can walk again."

Jonathan's heart sank, and his knees collapsed on the floor. "All I ever desired was to provide a comfortable and bright future for my family. But to do so at the expense of my son and those who are under my employ? I shouldn't have asked him to investigate farm two." He shook his head in dismay and shuttered. "What did I do?"

Mary ran to her husband's side. "No darlin'. Don't go blaming yourself. Remember, God opened these doors for us. You couldn't have foreseen this, but He knew all along. You must hold to your faith, Jonny." She squeezed his shoulders and quoted Romans 8:28. "And we know that all things work together for good to them that love God, to them who are the called according to his purpose."

Dr. Cassidy snapped his finger and turned abruptly to fetch his patient's accouterments shoved on a corner table. "I meant to give you Samuel's belongings. Upon removing his coat, I found these things tucked inside. Perhaps they may bring clarity on his discoveries at farm two." He placed the items into the grieving father's hands.

"DARNEL SEEDS." Jonathan read the burlap sack's labels and counted the other pieces. "Four bloodied bandanas. This is the evidence we need."

"Along with Huang-Fu's testimony, we can put those men behind bars." Mary's eyes enlarged.

Jonathan stood. "I agree, but even that won't help Samuel now. However, I will do everything in my power to avenge my son and those men assaulted. First, we must inform the marshal of our findings. Then second, gather the remaining Sower farmworkers and march over to S&S Farm to haul the wheat to the mill. I will not allow Harold and his men to handle my transactions."

"Good luck." Dr. Cassidy shook his head and grunted. "As I rolled my wagon off S&S Farm with Samuel lying unconscious in the bed, Harold and his men near booted me out and locked the swing gate behind me. A wall of hay bales and overturned wagons barricade the entrance now. It appears as if they are expecting retaliation of some sort. I even overheard them snickering and concocting an evil plan. Something about bringing the wheat to the mill, pocketing the money, and taking over the farm."

"Over my dead body, they will," Lad said. "I've got the right mind to go over there and shove my shootin' iron down their throats."

"Hang on now, son. We need to be one step above of these ruffians. The law must be on our side. I believe there are enough evidence and testimony here to lock them up and put a noose around their necks," Jonathan said. "Let's get the women and children home then head over to the courthouse. Would you mind meeting us there, doc? We sure could use your deposition."

"Sure. You can count on me to help."

"Ha," Jia-Li gasped. "Samuel just squeezed my hand." She bent her ear near his face. "I am here, darling."

The others hushed and gathered around Samuel's body, watching for any signs of movement. His lips quivered as his eyes rolled beneath his lids.

With every ounce of breath, Samuel forced a few staggered words out at a time. "P ... pushed." A groan passed his clenched teeth as everyone leaned in to listen. "Heard S&S superintendents. They attack farmworkers. Maxfield behind all."

Jia-Li's tears pearled on her husband's forehead. "Thank you, Lord, for this miracle. Samuel, you must live."

"That is a good sign, indeed. His mind is still intact." A relieved smile crossed Dr. Cassidy's face. "Pardon me, folks. Allow me to examine him while he is awake."

The family moved aside, making room. Jonathan held his trembling wife as the others watched with intensity.

The physician opened Samuel's eyelids. "I want you to focus on my hand and follow it." The disabled young man's eyes tracked as the doctor wiggled his fingers and drew air shapes.

"I'm going to work as fast as I can. Please respond by saying dull, sharp, or nothing as I check your sensory levels." Using the rounded end of a fibula, the physician brushed his patient's cheek. "What do you feel?"

"Dull."

Again he touched his face but with the safety pin's pointed end. "And now?"

Samuel's face twitched. "Sharp!"

The physician continued with brisk methodical precision throughout his patient's extremities as Samuel responded to every sensation. After the sensory evaluation, he moved on to the motor examination bending and flexing Samuel's arms and legs. The doctor's visage contorted into a hopeful grin as he completed the exam despite Samuel's groans of pain.

"Son, the Lord must be watching over you and sent an angel to your aide. The fall cracked your skull, and your back is badly injured. The miraculous news is that all your faculties are still remarkably spared. You must stay bedridden for several months. Other than that, you will be able to walk again and regain motility."

A whimper escaped as Samuel scanned the faces in the room and focused on his wife. "I love you, Jia-Li. Love y'all." He inhaled deeply, then unconsciousness reclaimed him again.

"All right. Let's let him rest. My wife will watch over him while we attend to matters before the marshal and the judge." Dr. Cassidy motioned the family to the front room and closed the examination room door. "You folks must be tired and famished. Why don't you go home and nourish yourselves, and I'll meet you men at the courthouse in say," he pulled out his timepiece from his vest pocket, "two hours?"

15

Evidence

Everyone in the courthouse turned their attention toward Jonathan as he, Huang-Fu, Lad, and Dr. Cassidy enter. The recent horrific events centered upon the town's two major wheat industries, which mortified the town's people. The news spread like rapid-fire through dry prairie brush. Curiosity plagued the room, and the onlookers draw close to witness firsthand the discourse to take place. Judge Wardly, Marshal Warner, and their deputies stood and extended compassionate greetings.

"We expected you to appear soon, Mr. Sower. Please take a seat all of you." The marshal motioned to a table and a group of chairs positioned by the judge's bench.

"We're going to need your help, sir. We discovered who our assailants are."

"Do tell. My men and I are frustrated with our lack of findings these past few weeks since your employee's incidents began. There must be a connection between their assaults and your son's ..." he gagged as if he had trouble saying the next word "... accident. How is Samuel doing, by the way?"

"We visited him at the clinic this mornin' after we arrived. Thank the Lord; he survived the fall. Now we pray after his back mends he will be able to use his arms and legs again. He awoke enough to tell us what he uncovered at S&S Farm."

Hoping to suppress his heavy despair, Jonathan inhaled. "Your Honor, can I approach your bench?"

"Yes, you may," Judge Wardly said as he relaxed into his seat and adjusted his black robe.

"Of all the years I've been plantin' wheat, weeds in my crop appeared only once durin' the initial breakin' up of the fallow ground. My Chinese farmworkers eradicated the thistles, and they never posed as a problem again. However, this season for the first time produced more than twenty-five percent of darnel." Jonathan passed a sample of faux wheat to the judge and continued.

"The difference this year is my acquisition of Frederick Maxfield's agriculture business. Because I purchased his industry so close to planting season, I had no choice but to hire his previous superintendents, Harold Jensen, Leonard Lambert, Grier Thomas, and Nevil Pierce. My better judgment warned me of their hostility toward my employment practices of utilizing Chinese labor. These men continue to communicate their anti-Chinese sentiments during our town's protest rallies." He glanced at Huang-Fu, who returned a nod.

Focusing on Lad, Jonathan press forward. "Peculiar and disheartening occurrences on S&S Farm, too many to mention, never ceased since this acquisition, which my son and son-in-law, can vouch for. They couldn't find proof of these superintendents' involvement … until a few days ago, Friday. I wired a telegram last week from Indiana to Samuel requesting him to be discreet and investigate my second farm because of the recent assaults to the Sower farmworkers whom I sent to assist with the new equipment."

Jonathan handed the marshal the empty burlap sack and the bloodied bandanas. "The doctor found these items hidden inside of Samuel's long coat."

The officer inspected the evidence and passed them on to the judge.

"Samuel discovered these things in the barn's loft at S&S Farm."

The weary farmer paced in front of the judge's bench. "Dr. Cassidy, my family, and I are witnesses to my son's testimony when he awoke. He said he overheard the four superintendents admittin' to their crime against the Sower Farm employees and that Frederick Maxfield commanded the heinous acts. When they discovered Samuel in the barn, they pushed him over the loft. The bloody bandanas are the masks they used to conceal their identity at the crimes they committed."

"I appreciate your testimony on Samuel's behalf, Mr. Sower, and the evidence you've provided. I consider these items as circumstantial because your son's direct deposition is needed in court to be certain these four men are our culprits. Since he is incapacitated and more than one person witnessed his testimony, I will accept your concession."

Jonathan straightened his stance and addressed the magistrate. "I would like to call on two witnesses. The first is my butler, Huang-Fu Suen."

The nervous yet eager employee stepped in front of the judge's bench and bowed.

"Please explain to Judge Wardly your recent revelation."

"Your Honor, you may recall over a year ago when three men wearing bandanas over their faces assaulted me on Merced Falls Road. Before I fell unconscious from the pain of my beating, I put to memory what happened that horrible day. The voices of these men are distinct, they mentioned the name Maxfield, and most identifiable of all, I remember snakes engraved on the heel bands of one of those men's boots." Huang-Fu paused, and sweat beaded on his brow as his hands and body shook from the recollection.

"Would you like a chair, sir? Continue when you are ready," the judge said.

"No, I am fine, Your Honor." He inhaled and let out a slow exhale. "A few months ago, my employer hosted a staff luncheon before leaving for his youngest son's wedding in Indiana. For first time I met his new employees from Sower and Sons Farm. Their voices sounded familiar to me. I did not make the connection until I retrieved my fork I drop beneath the table, and Mr. Harold's boot heel bands caught my attention. He wore the same boots with the same engraved snakes as the man who assaulted me. This was when the recollection of that day came back. The superintendent's voices, laughter, and their mention of Mr. Maxfield matched perfectly to those of the evil thugs. I have no doubt these are the men who attack me."

"Very well, Mr. Suen. Sharing this moment must be difficult indeed. Thank you for your testimony. You may be seated," the judge said. "Bring your next witness, Mr. Sower."

"I would like to call up Dr. Richard Cassidy," Jonathan said as the physician stood in front of the judge's bench. "Please share your findings, doctor."

"Your Honor, Leonard called me to tend to Samuel Sower's accident at S&S Farm. Upon arrival at the barn, I found the young man crumpled on the ground and the four superintendents, Harold, Leonard, Grier, and Nevil, hovering over him.

"As I conducted a cursory examination, Mr. Jensen dismissed the other three men as he waited for my prognosis. He appeared quite nervous and jittery to me and expressed more concern for Samuel's chances of surviving. When I explained to him that Samuel might not live, his countenance brightened rather than express consternation. He helped me carry his employer on a stretcher to my wagon and, with intent eagerness, escorted me off the farm.

"I became distracted by a wall of hay bales and turned over wagons being erected by the three superintendents as we approached the entrance. As I drove past the gate, Harold commanded Grier to bolt it shut. I stopped my wagon behind one of the oaks to make adjustments to Samuel's comfort. This was when I spied the four men standing behind the hay bales discussing plans of hauling the wheat to the mill, keeping the money for themselves, and taking control of the farm. I realized they built the wall for a retaliatory gunfight.

"At my clinic, I found the burlap sack and bandanas tucked in the inner pocket of Samuel's long coat after I removed his clothing for a full examination. If I had I not operated on his skull and let out some blood, the pressure would have killed him. Samuel, for the first time since his fall a few days ago, regained consciousness today when his family arrived. I too, can testify to his confession."

"Thank you, doctor. Please take a seat," the judge said. "Mr. Sower, you may provide a closing statement."

"Yes, Your Honor." Jonathan stood before the bench. "Common knowledge amongst the Snelling residents can attest to Frederick Maxfield and his former employee's hatred of the Chinese.

Their prejudices are evident in their employment practices, whereas Mr. Maxfield would rather hire white employees from another town than utilize the well qualified Chinese labor residin' in Snelling."

Clasping his hands behind him, Jonathan paced, choosing his words with caution. "Not only is Sower Farm a leadin' competitor to Maxfield Farm, but we continue to be the largest agricultural employer of Chinese farmworkers. To further aggravate this man's deep-seated animosity toward my enterprise, his recent health issues forced him to liquidate his business, which I acquired almost a year ago, and more than probable irks him to no end."

He stopped to make eye contact with the judge to assure the delivery of his message. "I believe the culmination of his atrocious loathin', unfortunate stroke, and business losses motivates him to instigate violent and desperate acts upon those he detests. Toward me in particular by way of destroyin' my property and disablin' my employees, and now family members. The apparent commonality with the recent assaults in our community is that the victims are the Chinese farmworkers under my employ, except my son, who is also a Sower Farm employee.

"Your Honor, as a law-abiding citizen of Snelling and contributor to its growin' success, I would hope justice would prevail on those who perpetrate crimes against me, my trade, which is the livelihood of others, my employees, and my family. The evidence and testimonies given to you this day prove, without a shadow of a doubt, that those who committed the recent assaults and destruction to my crops are the works of the instigator, Frederick Maxfield. The heinous acts were carried out by his former laborers and now current superintendents of Sower and Sons Farm, Harold, Leonard, Grier, and Nevil." Jonathan returned to his seat.

"Thank you for your testimonies. The court is adjourned for a forty-five-minute recess. I will provide the verdict when we reconvene." The judge stood and disappeared into an adjacent office, and the courtroom buzzed with anxiety anticipating the judge's decision.

16

Justice

"All rise," the deputy said as Judge Wardly returned and approached his bench. Those in the room stood and sat down as the magistrate adjusted himself in his seat. "Court is now in session."

"Thank you for your closing remark, Mr. Sower. The testimonies of the two witnesses, Huang-Fu Suen and Dr. Richard Cassidy are the direct proof needed to link the circumstantial evidence, the burlap sack and bandanas, and Samuel Sower's proxy testimony by his father Jonathan Sower, to the murder of one china man, the aggravated assault of nine others including Huang-Fu Suen and Samuel Sower, and the destruction of Jonathan Sower's property by the planting of tares in his fields. Those who executed these crimes are Frederick Maxfield, Harold Jensen, Leonard Lambert, Grier Thomas, and Nevil Pierce. I shall issue a warrant for their arrest forthwith. Upon their apprehension, each will receive the hanging sentence to be appropriated the following morning at the Second Garrotte oak tree in Groveland."

Those in the courtroom gasped as the judge continued. "In addition, Frederick Maxfield's estate is to be seized and awarded to Jonathan Sower as recompense for damages to his property, family, and staff. The current deed under Mr. Maxfield's possessorship shall be revoked and reassigned to Jonathan Sower at the close of this day." Judge Wardly slammed his gavel. "This meeting is adjourned. The court is dismissed."

Relief flooded Jonathan's being. All he held dear to him would once again be safe. Between himself, the marshal, deputies, Huang-Fu, Lad, the doctor, and a well-groomed banker, they exchanged somber handshakes and temperate back slaps for the justifiable payment, all the while considering the overall disheartening situation.

"My posse and I will serve these warrants first thing this afternoon, Mr. Sower. We don't want any murderers on the loose now, do we?" A gold tooth glistened under the marshal's mustache.

"I am ever so grateful for your service, marshal." Jonathan paused as a thought crossed his mind. "You men be careful. Harold and his boys are armed and anticipatin' a gunfight."

"Don't you worry about us. We can handle those hooligans."

"Pardon my askin', but how soon can I access farm two? The wheat needs to go to the mill before the heads spoil. Timin' is critical."

"You may take the property the moment we arrest these desperados. I'll send word to you after they are locked up. The county clerk will make sure the deed to the land and farmhouse is in your hands before you leave."

"What about Maxfield? Can you incarcerate a man with paralysis?"

"Sure, we can. Now he can experience the back of a hard wagon bed while incapacitated. By tomorrow mornin', his comfort won't matter anyway. Besides, he lost that privilege the moment he became an outlaw." The marshal shook his head. "Justice is swift and is served!" He winked, turned, then he and his posse collected their rifles and exited the courthouse eager to execute the judge's sentence upon the culprits at S&S Farm.

Before Jonathan could gather his belongings, a deliberate encounter appeared before him gesturing to meet his acquaintance. "Mr. Sower, may I have a moment of your time. My name is Mr. Goldwater, and I oversee the mortgage loans in our town."

Shrugging his shoulders and with reluctance, Jonathan returned a weak handshake, unsure of this person's intentions.

"Sir, you have saved the bank from further collections and imprisonment of Mr. Maxfield. We extended him grace beyond measure and were prepared to grant him added mercy by reducing his financial obligations due to his failing health. However, my clerk notified me of his distasteful and unfair business practice toward his employee, Mr. Lambert, who had borrowed a significant amount of money from Mr. Maxfield. If the loan weren't paid, the old man threatened to have his worker jailed.

"Upon hearing this, the bank's board renounced their generosity and were about to enforce the same justice that he offered his employee by arresting him and repossessing his assets. We can't be more pleased to hear Judge Wardly's verdict and sentence today. Unfortunately for Mr. Maxfield, consequent to death, his life insurance shall cover all debts, and the farmhouse and land will be free and clear for its new owner. You, Mr. Sower." With a wide grin and firm grip on the new wheat baron's elbow, the banker ended the conversation. "Please let me know if ever we can be a service to you." As quickly as he appeared, he rebounded to his post in the vault room downstairs.

Jonathan returned to his home with Huang-Fu and Lad as he clutched the new deed. The deputy's arrival pressed heavy on his mind in anticipation of the incarceration of Maxfield and the superintendents. His spirit danced inside him overjoyed by the judge's verdict and the award given to him to claim full rights of Sower and Sons Farm. However, the final hours, which was soon to unfold, tempered his joy.

"YOU BOYS HIDE BEHIND THEM OAKS and boulders while I approach the gate," the marshal said as the deputies positioned themselves to avoid becoming a bullet's target. "Be sure to cover me should this become ugly."

A few yards beyond the gated entrance bearing the insignia of Sower and Sons Farm, the officer recognized the hay bale walls and overturned wagons Dr. Cassidy described in court. Tucked between the bales' layers, four rifle barrel tips protruded aimed at him.

What a darn shame. The prestigious acreage glimmered in autumn's most exceptional colors from the lowering sun's golden beams, which backlit the yellowing oak leaves and illuminated the wheat bundles scattered about the harvested fields. However, the terror of these four culprits and their hate-filled mentor now cast a dark veil around the land. But not for long.

Using extreme caution as he approached the entrance on his horse, the marshal's heart pounded hard, forcing adrenaline throughout his limbs as he held his rifle tight under his arm. "Frederick Maxfield, Harold Jensen, Leonard Lambert, Grier Thomas, and Nevil Pierce … you are all wanted for the murder of one Chinaman, the aggravated assault of nine others including Huang-Fu Suen and Samuel Sower, and the destruction of Sower Farm property. I have a warrant for your arrest, and you all are to be sentenced tomorrow morning at Second Garrotte's hanging tree in Groveland. Drop your weapons and come out with your hands raised above your heads."

Elongated seconds passed when a fire blasted from the hay wall and braised the marshal's right shoulder. The horse reared up as the injured official moved with the saddle to keep from falling. Pulling the reins, he turned his mount about and directed the frighten beast behind one of the deputy's buckboards as a ration of ammunition sailed the air from both sides.

Bullets riddled the tree trunks, boulders, and wagons as well as shattered gaping holes in the bales. Bodies moved about behind the wall as the bales' integrity disintegrated.

"Let's smoke them out," said the marshal. "Jamison, Davis, mount your horses and torch the hay and carts. The rest of you cover them."

The two deputies rode their steeds with stealth to the front gate and flung their fiery torches at the dry, scattered straw. Within seconds flames immerse the barrier and spread rapidly to the bullet beaten wagons as the remaining officers' bullets continued to pelt the conflagration.

Screams penetrated the dense smoke as four men became inflamed, and shots pound their flesh.

Activity desisted from behind the wall.

"Ceasefire, men," the marshal said. Silence dominated the atmosphere except for the ringing in his ears caused by the blast of wailing gun balls. "Jamison and Ryan, go check the premises."

On foot, the deputies held their rifles to their eye and edged their way to the entrance. Not one shot flew toward them as they fired upon the lock and unlatched the gate. They drew themselves near the fallen bodies behind the inflamed walls and kicked them. Bullet-ridden and scarcely alive, the four supervisors screamed with pain. With immediacy, the officials handcuffed each of the ailing men regardless of their battered condition. Turning toward the officer in charge, Ryan waved his hands to signify the culprits' capture.

"Looks like there'll be a hanging tomorrow." The marshal rubbed the sweat off his forehead then put pressure on his shoulder's wound. "The rest of you put out the fire. Let's finish this job and arrest Maxfield."

The deputies extinguished the inferno, loaded the superintendents into the paddy wagons, and then proceeded to the farmhouse where the stroke-ridden former wheat baron still resided.

Serenity posed itself at the house as a striking contrast to the entrance's battlefield. Perched on the front porch rocker, the nurse awaited their arrival. She approached the marshal and his horse. "Sir, Mr. Maxfield is upstairs."

Warner tipped his hat. "Thank you, ma'am. One of my deputies will escort you home."

"No need. My carriage is in the barn. I expected this day to come." The layers of her petticoat, frumpy day dress, and greying apron whirled around her as she sauntered away, calm and unshakened by the harrowing event.

THE OFFICERS DISMOUNTED, proceeded to the farmhouse, climbed the stairs, and entered the flailing man's chambers. Frederick Maxfield said not one word and closed his eyes as the marshal announced his sentencing.

The deputies moved the paralyzed man on a stretcher, carried him to the wagon and laid him next to one of the supervisors. Maxfield turned his head to identify the blood-soaked former employee next to him. The repugnant smell of burnt flesh and clothing sent acidic nausea out of his sloped mouth. A faint mutter transpired from his lips. "Jensen."

A tear fell, and soon Maxfield's body began convulsing out of control.

The nurse pulled up in her carriage, peered at her former employer, and glanced at her timepiece. "Hmm, its pass his next dose of medication. But that won't even help him now." She fixated her sight on the marshal and waited for instruction. He shook his head side-to-side. She returned a nod, flicked the reins, and rambled away.

Gasps and gurgling came from the ill-fated land baron's throat and chest. The trepidation from the day's event spread over the deep crevices on his face.

A vision of the superintendents hovering over Samuel's crumpled body streamed in the marshal's mind as he and his men surrounded the man whose hatred-filled breath sputtered from his depleted body.

"Should we do something, sir?" Jamison ask.

"You heard the nurse. Nothing will help him. His guilt is going to be the death of him, and no medication can remove his sin and anxiety. Life and salvation are between him and God now."

Frederick Maxfield's chest rose and deflated with each shortened breath. Fear enveloped his eyes, and a drool soaked frown engulfed his discolored face.

"Well, it appears you have an appointment with the Second Garrott oak tree tomorrow, Mr. Maxfield." The head official said, then turned to his men. "Let's go drop these outlaws off at the Groveland jail to await their hanging, boys. Our work is done here."

Marshal Warner pulled a quirlie from his coat pocket, lit one end, and inhaled a long drag from the other. "Ryan, notify Jonathan Sower he can access his farm now."

17

Like Home

Jonathan, his family, and staff gathered in earnest by his desk, waiting for the news. When the rap came, he bolted from his seat and quick-stepped to the foyer. The door flung open, and his eyes settled upon the soot-covered Ryan. "Please, come into my office, deputy." Everyone's attention focused on the officer as he removed his hat.

"Mr. Sower, sir. You may now take claim of your property, formerly owned by Frederick Maxfield on the southwest end of Snelling. The four superintendents were apprehended after a difficult gun battle and hay bale inferno. As for the previous owner, his conscience's guilt betrayed him, and his heart near failed upon his arrest. They are scheduled to be hanged tomorrow morning at Second Garrotte in Groveland." Deputy Ryan extended a handshake.

A flurry of emotions enveloped the leading wheat baron of the western states. "Thank you, officer. I don't know if I should dance or hold a candle vigil. Please give Marshal Warner and your comrades our deepest gratitude for their unfailin' duty and bravery to uphold the law. I do pray this unfortunate fiasco did not harm any of them."

"The marshal will be nursing an injured shoulder for a few weeks, and we deputies will be mending our wagons. Thank the Lord; no lives were lost on our side. I will inform them of your appreciation.

Good evening to you all." Ryan winked, placed his hat on his head, and found his way out.

"I guess a large basket of pabulum is in order for each of those men. Shall we get to work, ladies?" Mary's steady voice reflected her appeasement and broke the stupefied cloud that rested upon the Sower household.

Optimistic affections reciprocated amongst the family and staff. The jovial women locked arms and swirled away to the kitchen, hurling aspirations to make baked goods and confections as the men directed their attention to Jonathan for his instruction.

"I believe we have our work cut out for us at S&S Farm. Yung, Sheng-Li, and Anguo, please notify the farmhands to haul the wheat to the mill tomorrow, while Lad and I make plans to refit the farmhouse. Mary and I have decided that the house will be Samuel and Jia-Li's new home for their growing family. I will hire a nurse while he convalesces and their own household staff. We shall leave at dawn."

SEVERAL WAGONS DRIVEN BY JONATHAN and his superintendents rolled past the char remains of buckboards and hay bales just beyond the gate archway at Sower and Son's Farm. Spent bullets on the ground glistened in the morning light. The men must clean this up before the women come calling. First impressions are lasting, and this place must feel like home for my son and his family.

Aside from the disturbing entrance, the tranquil beauty of the immense property lay untouched and in order. The wheat bundles scattered about the land were ready to be hauled away to the mill and the heads ground into fine flour. His seasoned superintendents and farmhands needed no instruction and proceeded to the field as he and Lad moseyed forward.

When the farmhouse came into view, Jonathan strained to imagine Samuel and Jia-Li relaxing on the porch as his future grandchildren romped on the front lawn. Lord, I do pray for your blessings upon this property and for Samuel's full recovery. Please allow him to walk again and fulfill his role as heir to my estate.

Lad brought the wagon to a halt, and the two men dismounted and entered the home. The air wreak of stale cigars, and the homely interior begged a woman's touch. His mind took mental notes of items and fixtures that needed mending, removal, and replacement.

"Pa. This way to the office." His son-in-law opened the door into a dingy, dark room bestowed with walnut stained floors and a massive mahogany desk. Against the back wall stood a black Mosler safe trimmed with gold lettering and pinstripes.

Jonathan fumbled with its lock, but the seal did not budge. "We'll need to get a safecracker to open this piece of work." He continued to sift through files until he came across an accounting ledger dated one year earlier before his purchase of the Maxfield wheat business. "Ah. This will be interestin' readin' material. Not that it matters."

They marched upstairs and visited each of four lackluster rooms saving the master chamber for last. Frederick's unkempt sheets evoked the upheaval that took place only yesterday.

"This bedroom furniture and all Maxfield's clothing are the first items to be removed, Lad. We'll want as few recollections of him as possible if none at all in this place.

"Once the home's renovations are complete, I will request for Pastor McSwan to come over to pray for God's cleansing and blessing upon the property, the business, our family, the entire household, and livestock."

"Yes, sir. And how about we open the windows and let this house breathe? It can use some fresh air and sunlight."

"I agree. Let's do that, and then we can decide what furnishings to keep and what to sell. Once the heavy lifting is done, I'll have the women come and administer their refinements. We shall transform this house into what it was meant to be … a home filled with love, joy, and well-being."

SIX AGONIZING WEEKS of initial recovery allowed Samuel enough strength to be moved out of the doctor's clinic to his new home.

"Ugh. Remind me to patch every bump on Snelling Road when I'm walkin' again." He chuckled, trying to make light of his temporary paralytic condition as his father brought the wagon to a halt at Sower and Son's Farm.

"That's the spirit, son. Keep thinkin' forward. You'll be workin' in no time," Jonathan said as the exuberant father jumped in the back with the three Sower Farm superintendents to where Samuel sat in a Bath wheeled chair strapped firm to the wagon's floorboards so as not to move around.

"Gentle now, fellas." His father placed his hands on one of the wooden arms, Anguo the other, while Yung stood behind and Sheng-Li in front to guide the wheels down the ramp. "Are you ready, son?"

Samuel nodded.

"Okay, on the count of three, let's roll him down. One, two, three." From the back of the wagon, the men rolled him and the wheeled chair to the ground. "All right. Let's take him upstairs to the master's chamber."

Jonathan patted his shoulder. "Welcome to your new home, son."

A tear trickled from the corner of Samuel's eye as his very pregnant wife waved from the porch of the freshly painted farmhouse. Next to her stood his mother, sisters, brother-in-law, a nurse, and a new domestic staff he had never met before—all bowed or curtsied. A month and a half had passed since he last stepped foot on this property. And now it was his to live in and manage … a thought he still struggled to grasp.

Samuel recalled a few weeks earlier while he recovered at the doctor's clinic, his father explaining the judge's decision and the horrific confrontation that took place between the marshal and his deputies with Maxfield and his outlaws. His father's information bent like a fairy tale dream in his pain medicated stupor. The restitution deemed more than he could ever imagine.

"Welcome home, my love," Jia-Li said. She touched his hand as he pushed past her.

He returned a smile. "My home is wherever you are, darlin'."

As the men rolled him into the home and carried him in his chair up the stairs, Samuel gawked at the transformation. Beams of sunlight cascade through the window's lacy curtains illuminating the interior. The country-style furnishings were casual and charming compared to the dark hand-carved wood furniture of its previous owner. Fresh cut lavender, sage, and roses grace the foyer, and its fragrance filled the air giving chase to any lingering tobacco redolence.

Anxiety gripped him as they approached the master's chamber from thoughts of Maxfield in this room, bedridden from a stroke. Now he suffers a similar fate because of this man. His spine ached at the thought.

The butler opened the door, and the same sweet floral fragrance and paint met him. Flowers from well-wishers filled the room. The familiar bedroom set he purchased for him and Jia-Li now occupied the room positioned to face the window rather than parallel as before. Light wispy curtains replaced the heavy brocade ones and moved with the warm, supple autumn breeze that circulated the interior. Framed tintypes of he and his bride on their wedding day displayed on their dresser brought about pleasant and joyful memories.

However, the item that would change his perspective of this house, pillared next to their bed. Its presence announced a future hope, a means to erase the former resident's anamnesis and usher forth a new beginning—all attention clamor to its glowing draw. Resembling a beacon of light stood a baby bassinet dressed in a white cotton skirt and endowed with a feather cushion and handmade quilt embroidered with sentiments from his mother and sisters. The first grandchild to carry the Sower name will share and enlighten their bedroom until weaned. Then he or she would find respite in the adjoining nursery room.

"Set him on the bed, men," Jonathan said. "On the count of three. One, two, three." The men lifted Samuel off the chair and perched him on his mattress.

Jia-Li fluffed the pillows at his back. "Darling, I hope you are pleased." She leaned over and kissed him, then combed through his ruffled hair with her fingers.

"You truly outdid yourselves. Your renovations have exceeded you all. Thank you for preparing a warm and pleasant return."

His mother stood near him, pulling a robust middle-aged woman beside her. "Oh, my darlin' son. I thank God every day that you are with us. In due time your healin' will be complete. I'd like you to meet Agatha. She is your nurse and will be assistin' you with daily therapeutic exercises to help you walk again."

"How do you do, Mr. Sower? I believe you, and I will become well acquainted with each other for the next few months." She reached down and squeezed his legs. "Strong muscles indeed. Won't take long. You'll soon be running circles around your children."

"Also, meet our domestic help," Jia-Li said. "Ah Chum, our butler and housekeeper, Ah Hie, our cook, Ah Yow, our gardener, and Ah Teny, our handyman." The men bowed from the foot of the bed.

"The pleasure is mine. I look forward to the days ahead of us. I'm at your mercy. However, I do not plan on remaining like this for long. I'm made of strong Sower stock. This body is meant to be plowin', sowin', and harvestin' the fields."

"Oh." The exuberant young mother-to-be gasped and rubbed her abdomen. "I think our baby agrees with you." She sat next to him and placed his hand on the active bundle inside her. "This little one will make sure of it, indeed."

Laughter filled the room.

"All right. I think it's time we give my son some rest. He's had an arduous day. Much we take for granted. I recall my days of recuperation after the war," Jonathan said.

"I shall bring your supper, shortly," Ah Hie said as everyone left the room.

"Please stay, darlin'. Your presence comforts me." Samuel held Jia-Li's hand.

Returning a warm and assuring smile, she said, "Yes, my love. I will never leave you."

18

Letters

"I'm headed to the post office. Does anyone need anythin' from town?" Naomi donned her cape and bonnet in the foyer as she waited for an answer from her parents and the household staff on a damp November Tuesday afternoon. The raindrops that pound the front porch roof did not minify her pursuit for happiness. William Tyne was faithful to send her bi-weekly letters. She would go every day to fetch them if need be. However, the train delivered rural mail on Tuesday and Friday only.

Her mother trod down the stairs with a letter in hand. "You're a regular postal customer these days since our return from Indiana. You and Mr. Tyne send each other posts like clockwork. Do I detect a long-distance relationship blossomin'?"

Naomi felt a rush of warmth to her face as she tied a bow beneath her chin. "Ma, you're the one who insisted I keep knocking on God's door and request a husband right for me. I guess I should've been more specific and asked that he be a resident of California."

"Well, I suppose if Pa and I are acceptin' of David findin' his spouse in Indiana, we cannot hold a double standard and not allow you to do the same. William does seem to be a fine and well established young man. I pray that he is a godly one too. From the way you both fixated on each other on the dance floor at David's weddin', I'd say God made a match from heaven."

"He sure did, Ma, in more ways than one. And yes, he is a God-fearin' man." Her lips quiver a grin. "Havin' a long-distance relationship has its advantages. We have no choice but to communicate and share about ourselves. I believe you and Pa will adore him. Oh, Ma, I miss him and long for him in a terrible way."

Mary straightened the bow on Naomi's bonnet then hugged her. "Oh my darlin' daughter, I'm so happy you've found love. However, I'm not sure if this is what your pa and I would want for you. I insist you consider the consequences should the two of you decide to become more serious. It may require one of you havin' to relocate. I doubt that William plans on givin' up his lucrative corn farm. It's too valuable an asset to the Indianans." Mary brushed an unruly curl from Naomi's brow. "And you, my dear, are too great an asset for your pa and me. I don't know what I'll do without you. We need you here on our farms, especially now that we have two to manage. Must you pursue this relationship?"

A sudden burst of heat welt up in Naomi's belly, much like a canning pot that was to explode from pressure. She could not believe the words that came from her mother's lips. *How could Ma and Pa make such a request when they know how much I long for a husband? As much as I love this farm and my parents, I will not allow it or them to dictate my chance for a happy marriage.*

Naomi chewed on her bottom lip to avoid spewing hurtful words. A quick glance at the farmhouse's foyer and the doors that lead to its many memory filled rooms, caused her to cringe at the possibility of leaving the only home she has known since living in Kentucky. She pulled away from her mother's grasp and felt her hands tremble from the dose of reality, which avails at that moment. This thought never occurred to her during the last two months of conglomerations with her new beau. She had no words to express her torn sentiments.

Her mother broke the awkward silence. "My heart tells me it may be me running to the post office twice a week in the near future to fetch letters from Indiana. Not only from David but from you too? At least I know David and Clara are committed to returnin' to Snelling after he gets his degree." Mary fumbled with her envelope. "I think I miss you already and you haven't even left yet. My prayer is that William would want to move to California."

Naomi's throat tightened, and she returned a warm hug as her mother's eyes watered. Her mother's acceptance of her courtship with William is the assurance she needed to move forward with life's new possibilities.

"Oh, Ma, let's not get too far ahead of ourselves. I'll be sure to give you plenty of notice if our relationship escalates and requires relocation for either one of us. William and I have only just begun to get acquainted with one another. There is no talk of marriage yet."

Her mother cocked her brow and returned an expression that lacked confidence in her last statement. "Well, can I count on you, for now, to mail this letter to David for me? He and Clara have been diligent to pray for Samuel's full recovery and are anxious to hear any news."

"Of course, Ma." Naomi tucked the parchment envelope in her cape pocket next to her rose-scented letter for William. "I'll be back before the sun sets." She kissed her mother's cheek, grabbed an umbrella, and headed out the door where Anguo had the horse and carriage ready at the wayside path.

Cozied aboard the carriage, Naomi called out with eager anticipation, "Walk on!" The horse pulled forward with a gallant trot toward the town's post office where her beloved's communique await.

UPON HER RETURN HOME, Naomi parked the carriage in the barn, opened her umbrella, and scurried to the house, avoiding puddles along the way. Drenched, she removed her bonnet and cape, pulled the travel-weary envelope from her pocket, and shuffled into the living room. A warm hearth fire and the wing back chair gave a beckoned glow. She sat down, and her cold fingers clamored to open the letter and read its content.

My dearest Naomi,
Good news indeed to hear of your brother's progress. Surely he must be

anxious to put his hand to the plow at the newly acquired farm and also desire to walk before his child is able. I will continue to include him in my prayers.

The corn harvest is completed, my farm is once again hush, and I find myself rummaging for projects to keep from idling. However, I cannot wrap my mind around work when all I can think of is you, my dear. With Christmas fast approaching, my heart longs more and more to be near you. The thought occurred to me to visit you and your family in December during the off-season. I can rent a room in Snelling, and return to my farm after the New Year. This would allow us plenty of time for a better acquaintance. Please discuss this with your family. I do not want to put them out in any way. And I will only visit upon your request.

> *With tender regards,*
> *William Tyne*

The warmth from the fire only flickered compared to the joyful enthusiasm emanating from within her. Her cold hand's lavender shade turned a sultry rosy ivory from the exuberant thought of time spent with the man of her dreams. December, Christmas. He will be here sitting next to me, warming himself by this fire, dining with my family, strolling these very grounds.

Her eyes peered down at her muddy boots and her skirts' rain-soaked hem. Oh, Lord! What will I wear? I am in no way ready for a man to come calling!

19

Which Path?

Naomi paced by the parlor window as she fidgeted with her bustled wool skirt and ruffled blouse. On this day, she spied often through the lacy curtains toward the wayside path for any sign of her brother-in-law's carriage.

"You are your father's daughter," her mother said from her winged-back chair by the warm hearth while sipping on hot tea. "Please sit down. Relax before you wear yourself thin, and you won't have any energy left to entertain your beau this evenin'."

Ignoring her mother, Naomi tried to adjust her corset from above her clothing and inhale deep. "I can barely breathe with this dreaded cage about my chest. I'd be like a cockatoo bobbin' on a perch if I were to sit down." She centered the cameo pinned to the collar of her shirt. "I do pray once William is settled in and we are past the formalities, I shall introduce him to the bona fide Naomi Sower, and he can witness for himself my abilities."

"He will need to sojourn longer than a month to capture the refinements of you, my dear." Her father entered the room with his clay pipe and tobacco tin in hand. Ensconced in the chair across from her mother, he packed his smoking apparatus, lit it, and puffed on its sweet, hearty aroma.

"Pa, I'll take that as a compliment, for I do not see myself as a complicated person. I conceal no trickery about me." Naomi smirked. "Truth be told, I attribute all my skills and knowledge to the great farmin' masters themselves, you and Ma. For that, I am forever grateful."

"Daughter, you need not fret. Any good farmer will know a good catch when he sees one." Jonathan winked at Mary.

"Oh, Jonny. Ya make me blush." Her mother giggled like a teenage school girl.

"Pa, it was mighty intuitive of you to send Lad to fetch William at the Snelling Hotel."

"Well, it was simple math, really—a process of elimination. As your chaperones, your ma and I need to be here to welcome William into our home and keep an eye on matters. We knew you'd be preoccupied with preparin' yourself for his arrival. Sure enough, Samuel or Jia-Li are in no condition to do so. And Sarah's hands are full with the children. That leaves Lad as the perfect candidate." Jonathan grinned and sucked on his pipe, letting out puffs of smoke.

"Perhaps Lad can shed some brother-in-law insight and calm some of William's apprehensions too. I am most certain your young man is in a state of a quandary as much as you are. Wouldn't you agree, Jonny?"

"Of course. He wouldn't be human if he weren't."

"Well, I can't stand this waitin'. I'm goin' to see if Liang can fix an herbal tea to calm my nerves." Naomi peered out the window once more then darted into the kitchen and away from her parents' irritating counsel, although they meant well.

THE KNOCK CAME TO THE FRONT DOOR. Naomi near dropped her cup into its saucer as she idled her time scanning the San Joaquin Argus's articles.

"Miss Naomi, would you care for some more tea?" Liang asked.

"No, thank you. There isn't enough time. Lad and William are already here. The valerian root and chamomile did me right to remove some anxiety, though. I hope my knees stop knockin' together." She let out a nervous sniggle. "Please, pray for me."

Naomi stood and straightened the wrinkles from her attire. She identified her parent's voices answering the door.

"Welcome to our home, Mr. Tyne," her mother said.

"Thank you, Mrs. Sower. Please, address me as William. I've been looking forward to this day for some time now."

"Oh, indeed. A certain young lady is mutually agreed," her father said. "Please allow our butler, Huang-Fu, to take your coat, men."

"Actually, Pa, I'm going to head back home to fetch Sarah and the children and will return with them later this evening to join all of you for supper. If that's all right with you," Lad said.

"Of course. I'm sure they are as anxious to reacquaint themselves with William as we are."

Her mother snickered. "We shall see you tonight with your family, Lad. Now William, why don't you relax in the parlor with Jonathan while I inform Naomi of your arrival and have Liang fetch some refreshments."

A FAINT ACHE BEGAN TO TROUBLE Naomi's stomach. Heat rose from her torso beneath the swaddling corset, leaving a thin layer of sweat to gather beneath her collar. Calm yourself, Naomi. Take a deep breath. Please, pain go away. Now is not the time to quarrel with an ulcer. Her head turned toward her mother as she entered the kitchen and closed the door behind her.

"Are you ready, dear?" Her mother clasped her shaking hand in hers. "William is quite anxious to see you. If I might add, he appears quite dashing in his woolen vested suit."

Naomi could only answer with a nod. She pictured her suitor as a knight in shining armor. The thought made her chuckle and brought her anxiety down a notch. Dear Lord, it must be the valerian root and chamomile. I pray I do not make a fool of myself and say or do something silly.

"Liang, please fetch some refreshments for us and bring it to the parlor," Mary said. "Shall we, daughter?"

Her mother's gentle nudge guide Naomi out of the kitchen and to the foyer where they paused before entering the parlor. Upon opening the door, she stood beneath its entry as her mother shadowed her.

Naomi's gaze locked with William's. He stood, and like a slow-moving magnet, he drew near to her. Standing inches from one another, his breath brush her face. His warm hands gathered hers and, with suppleness, brought them to his lips where he pressed a kiss upon them.

"Hello, my dear, Naomi." He took a slight step back to examine her. "You are as beautiful as I remember you."

Joy abundant fill her once aching abdomen. A torrent of sweet emotions rushed to her face. "Thank you, William. And you are as gallant and charming as I recall." Her feet seemed to hover as he led her to the parlor sofa across from her parents sitting in their wing-back chairs.

Her father began a casual conversation. "And how was your travel, William? I hope it wasn't too arduous."

"Far from that, sir. I found the locomotive ride very exhilarating. I didn't realize the vastness of our country—land beyond measure. I'm certain that as an agriculture farmer, you share the same vision as I when discovering virgin territory. A farmhouse surrounded by acres upon acres of cornfields somehow always comes into my view. However, this time that scenario includes a wife and children making merry alongside me."

William's dreamy demeanor moved from her father's direction to hers. He must have sensed her parent's awkward speechless disposition in response to his candor, for he was keen to change the subject. "I do hope for the opportunity to one day visit the Pacific Ocean. Much is spoken about it."

"What a splendid idea. In all our years residin' in California, we've yet to see the coastline," Naomi said. "Pa, can that be arranged? Not only can we see the ocean, but we can also explore San Francisco. A cable car system is the city's new mode of transportation. We can visit Ghirardelli's chocolate factory, have lunch at Fisherman's Wharf and stay at the recently opened Palace Hotel. The city must be spectacular durin' the holidays. Samuel and Jia-Li could not stop talking about that place."

Eyes enlarged, Mary gasped. "Sam, Jia-Li! We can't go. Our grandbaby is due any day now."

Jonathan scratched at his beard. "Well, perhaps we can find time after the baby is born. Let me look into it, and I will let you know my findin's. We've much to show William here in our hometown, and with Christmas around the corner, we may be short on time."

"Yes. The ocean will have to wait for another visit. I would love the grand tour of your fine Sower Farm's establishment. After all, that is why I am here to become more acquainted with all of you." He turned to Naomi with glowing intentions. "And especially the woman I've been courting long distance for the past few months.

"California found its place on the map for many promising agriculturalists back east. I'm one amongst those big dreamers." William grinned and relaxed into the sofa. "The thought of moving West has tickled my fancy for some time now. But no motivation beckons me to leave the comforts of the farm of my youth. Until now." His twinkling eyes connect with hers. "I inherited it after my parents' unfortunate death during the war. As much as I am bereaved with those memories, the farm holds special sentiments for me. To part with it would be most difficult."

Jonathan writhed in his chair. "We understand your dilemma all too well. Unlike your situation, we experienced the wars' horrific effects first hand when our farm in Kentucky became a hospital for many dyin' soldiers. That very reason is why we left our home for a fresh start in California. After much prayer and Godly counsel, we stepped out in faith and followed His callin'. The good Lord went before us and carved a path through many obstacles to get us to the station we are now. I must say, I do not regret that decision one bit."

"Truly, God's blessings are apparent through your faith and obedience. I pray the Lord makes my path clear." William reached over and squeezed her hand.

Naomi peered into William's eyes, hoping to find certainty. He loves his farm, yet he is willing to relocate for me. Will we marry now or wait till he makes a decision? How long shall that take? Lord, gettin' married is goin' to take longer than I imagined. What if he asks me to return to Indiana with him? Oh, Lord, is this your will for me?

The afternoon wane and the topic of their conversation skip about like a smooth flat rock skipping over gentle water. A few minutes after the foyer clock chimed five times, Huang-Fu opened the front door, and the Hampton family entered and made themselves at home. The children ran to their grandparents with Sarah and Lad behind them. Greetings were exchanged, and before anyone could make themselves comfortable, Liang entered the parlor and said with great pleasure, "Supper is ready."

20

Perfect in Weakness

The familiar aroma of stuffed roasted turkey, sweet potatoes, yams, green beans, and assorted pies graced the Sower farmhouse. The luscious scent wafted through the air to where Naomi stood starring at the harvested fields from the living room window. Memories of her maneuvering the harvester with her father and the farmworkers, corralling the mules and horses, and milking the cows during morning's wee hours play tug-of-war with anticipative marital visions to William Tyne at his faraway land in Indiana.

The sound of clinking dishes dash her reminisce moment and brought her forward to her current anxiety, and she began to reason with herself. *As much as I love Thanksgiving, I wish the next few days would be over with. William will be here soon, and my emotions tell me I'm still not ready. Is it proper for a woman to meet a man at the hotel where he is staying?*

No, of course not, Naomi! You should always bring a chaperone with you.

But who? Pa, Ma?

While envisioning William's cornfields, she twirled around her finger, a stray ringlet at her neck's nape. *What can life possibly be like on a corn farm? Can't be that much different. Winters may be longer* and colder, unlike here in California. The thought made her quiver. Who would have ever thought I'd be returning to the Eastern United States? Bitter cold winters and sweltering hot summers. It's no wonder any crops grow in that region. I must be moonstruck to want to move back there.

Is this what love is like, Lord? My mind can make no sense of it all. Yet Your Holy Spirit inside me tells me that William is the one for me. My heart also tells me so.

Footsteps from the foyer fast approached, and the living room door swung open. "Stop your day dreamin', Naomi, and give Liang and me a hand settin' the table." Her mother snapped. "Your sister and brother and their families will be arrivin' soon."

"Oh, all right, Ma. I'm comin'." She shuffled toward her mother, who dangled a brown and yellow plaid pinner apron before her. Naomi snatched the un-alluring domestic garb from the agitated woman's hand, pin it to her bodice as her mother tied a bow in the back, giving the straps a hardy tug.

"Ugh," Naomi expel a gasp of air from the sudden intense pressure signifying her mother's momentary perturbed disposition. "I apologize. So many things are on my mind to prepare myself before William gets here."

Her mother chuckled. "And you don't think I'm aware of that? Your mind has been a million miles away since he sent the letter telling you about his visit. I swear I've been talkin' to a sack of wheat just sittin' around waitin' to be useful."

"Oh, Ma. You know this is all new to me. I have no clue how to be courted. I'm not like Sarah, who naturally knows how to react to a man's needs. I'm just a country bumpkin."

"A beautiful and resourceful country bumpkin!" Her mother turned her around and pinched her cheek to make it rosy. "That is the reason why William loves you too. I'm sure he could pick any woman he wants bein' the successful farmer that he is. But he has someone specific in mind who would make him happy in more ways than one. Not every woman can do the things needed to live a farmin' lifestyle."

Fists on her hips and feet firm on the ground, her mother affirm William's decision making process with sound wisdom. "He is aware you come from good Sower stock raised with everythin' there needs to know about growin' crops and managin' a farm. He is one smart fella to have chosen you, darlin'."

"Oh, Ma. Your depiction of me is quite pretentious and hopeful at best. My mediocre social skills lack grace. Will you show me some proper courtin' etiquette and manners?"

"Of course I will, sweetheart. The Bible gives the best instruction for any aspirin' bride in Proverbs 31:10-31, 'The Virtuous Wife.' This chapter is a must to read. The last two verses sum all a woman needs to know to be her best, whether married or not. 'Favour is deceitful, and beauty is vain: but a woman that feareth the Lord, she shall be praised. Give her of the fruit of her hands; and let her own works praise her in the gates.'

"You need not worry. Just be yourself. You've been taught well." Mary fiddle with the loose hair strand at Naomi's nape and tuck it into the Victorian style bun resting atop her head. Her mother spun her around to evaluate her stature. "If he likes what he sees, then he'll stick around, and you won't have to live your life tryin' to be someone you aren't. If he leaves, then it wasn't meant to be, and you'd be spared heartache down the road.

"Remember, 'Trust in the Lord with all thine heart; and lean not unto thine own understanding,'" her mother began quoting their family's favorite life passage in Proverbs 3:4, 5, and 6.

Naomi finished her sentence with a sigh of relief, "In all thy ways acknowledge Him, and He shall direct thy paths."

"Now, the second advice I'll give you is to keep busy. Time will pass like greased lightnin' when your mind and body are occupied. Before you know it, the first of December will be upon you. Shall we start in the kitchen?"

Biblical encouragement from her mother always brought a sense of comfort and reliable assurance. She could always count on her mother's unfailing love for the Lord and His excellent precepts to provide her with sound guidance, which will glorify God. "Yes, Ma, lets."

Amongst the kitchen's hubbub, Jonathan heard both wagons approach and park in front of the farmhouse as he read the San Joaquin Argus by the hearth in his office. The faint sound of Samuel and Jia-Li's cheerful voices mingle with her father's Mandarin greetings, which flit around the yard like church bells ringing and then drift into the room. An immense joy reverberated in every part of his body, causing him to put the paper down and watch his family's arrival from the window.

"Easy, Mr. Samuel," Huang-Fu said. "Put your weight on my shoulder, and I will help you down from carriage."

A few muffled groans escape Samuel, then stopped. "Thank you, Huang-Fu."

"Here is your cane, my love," Jia-Li said.

"Thank you, dear. Now please be careful climbing out of the carriage too. You cannot see your feet, so let your father guide you down."

"Yes, I will."

"Take my hand, daughter. Do you feel the step?" Her father reached toward her.

She dangled her foot beneath her protruding abdomen covered in petticoat layers and a very loose maternity day dress. "Ah, there it is. Thank you, father." Her feet upon the ground, she then kissed her father's cheek. "I am so glad to be with you again."

The high pitch laughter of Jonathan's grandchildren clamoring out of their wagon, followed by Sarah and Lad's chastening pierced through Samuel and Jia-Li's exchange.

"Amanda, Billy, slow down before you fall and dirty your good clothes!" Sarah said.

"Children, listen to your mother." Lad disguised his low growl with gaiety.

Pitter patter of footsteps on the front porch and the nimble raps of small hands that pound the door announced his family's arrival.

"They're here!" Jonathan said, and he raced to the foyer as Mary, Naomi, and Liang hustle out of the kitchen behind him. Upon opening the door, they were greeted by two grinning cherubs.

"My grandbabies," Mary said and opened her arms.

"Nana and Papaw!" The children squealed and fell into Jonathan and Mary's embrace.

A glance into the yard, Jonathan and the ladies watched in awe as Samuel crept across the lawn one step at a time holding a cane in one hand and Isabelle's hand in the other. The pair struggled to coordinate their steps and resist any pain, which forged on their faces. Still in recuperation, Isabelle continued to regain her strength with a healthy diet and exercise, and daily regimented walks help to restore Samuel's back muscles. They are living miracles. A grin swept across Jonathan's face, ecstatic of their accomplishments.

Toes stopped short at the porch's first step, Samuel and Isabelle fixated on the challenge before them as distress lines topped their brows. Without a word, Samuel turned his focus upon his four-year-old niece, squeezed her hand, and flashed a reassuring and confident smile. They pushed forward with laborious effort, lifted each leg, and landed it with a thud upon each step. Every level called for rest and regroup as they climbed. Following close behind to brace them should they fall were Sarah, Lad, their very pregnant daughter-in-law, Jia-Li, and her father, Huang-Fu.

To reach the top of the porch might have been to climb the peak of Mount Everest. Both Samuel and Isabel were exhausted, breathing heavy with sweat on their foreheads.

"Welcome home, son," Jonathan said as he extended his arm to Samuel for him to grab. Samuel leaned on Jonathan as Lad carried Isabel. Jia-Li clung to her father's elbow, and the entire family filed into the farmhouse to extol in the year's achievements and give thanks.

What a beautiful sight to see. My remarkable family. Thank You, Lord, for your blessings.

Then the Lord's voice spoke clear in Jonathan's head, reminding him of 2 Corinthians 12:9, "My grace is sufficient for thee: for my strength is made perfect in weakness."

21

First Born

"You can relax now. We're here," Mary said, trying to make light of the anxious moment. She and Liang enter Jia-Li and Samuel's bedroom, where the expectant mother lay bearing down and writhed in pain. "Your gardener, Ah Yow, rushed to my home as fast as he could and informed me that Jia-Li began her labor. He was rather frantic because the doctor was not at his clinic. The doctor's butler said he had been called away to tend to a shootin' incident at one of the local cow ranches early this mornin'."

Mary placed a basket filled with aprons, linens, sheets, and syringes on the bed. A kiss upon her daughter-in-law's forehead, she then rubbed her swollen belly and presented a warm and comforting smile. "So your ma and I are goin' to deliver our grandchild into this world."

Fright filled Jia-Li's eyes while she clutched Sam's hand and let out a scream as the next labor pain reached its climax.

"Not to worry, daughter. Your mother-in-law has much experience. Remember, she had four children of her own, delivered Sarah's children, and also countless livestock." Liang held Jia-Li's other hand. "Follow her instructions while I fetch hot water kettle and basin."

Mary donned her apron, placed clean linens under Jia-Li's buttocks and pillows under her waist. After Liang returned with the items she needed, both women washed their hands, being careful to touch only Jia-Li and their soon-to-arrive grandchild.

"All right, dear," Mary said as she lifted Jia-Li's nightgown above her abdomen, "I need to assess the baby's position." She wrapped her warmed hands about the heaving mound with gentle pressure locating the babe's head and legs.

Oh, Lord, the child is breech. This will not be a simple delivery. Father, help us all. God's gift of knowledge swept through Mary's mind bringing to remembrance the birthing steps for feet-first babies. He provided the confidence she needed to proceed, and her actions followed His voice's instruction within her. "My dears, the baby's head is not where it should be."

"What?" Samuel's countenance fell, and his eyes locked with his mother's.

Jia-Li's body shook, and her sweat-soaked brow near press together. "No … no."

With soft strokes, Mary caressed her daughter-in-law's face and then her swollen belly to bring surety to the frightened young woman. "I will need to reposition the baby, so his head is at your pelvis, sweetheart."

"Have you done this before, Ma?" Samuel's face went flush.

The expecting parents' anxiety-riddled glances prompted Mary to soften her voice and nod with calm assurance as she held both their hands. "Yes, Sam, dear. I've delivered a few breech calves in my days. Surely, deliverin' a human child should be similar if not less complicated. Pray for the Lord's wisdom to guide me."

Liang began to whisper a silent prayer as she placed her hand upon her daughter's head. Her focus then turned to Mary. "What do you need me to do?"

"We'll need to work fast, Liang. There's a chance the baby's umbilical cord can get tangled and cut off the baby's circulation. For now, you must hold down Jia-Li's shoulders. First, I'll press the baby up away from her pelvis. The second step will be to rotate him to the side. Then finally, the last stage will be to position his head down."

Mary used one of the linens to wipe away the moisture on her daughter-in-law's forehead. "My dear girl. Will you trust me to bring you and the baby through this ordeal safely?"

Jia-Li shook her head. "Yes, mother, I must."

"All right. Then let us begin. This will be painful. Darlin' do your very best not to bear down while I turn your child." Mary rolled a cloth and placed it in Jia-Li's mouth. "Bite down on this when the pain comes. Are we all ready?" Her family nodded and gripped the shaking mother-to-be.

Mary positioned herself on the bed below Jia-Li and began a gentle push upward on her abdomen against the baby. Her daughter-in-law blared in pain and clutched her son's hand so tight that their palms turn white for lack of blood circulation. After several minutes Jia-Li loosened her grip while the pain subsided and she regained some strength.

"Two more steps to go," Mary said. "Ready?"

Jia-Li nodded as her tears intermingled with sweat.

Mary's hands move as if not her own. Calculated swift movements push and pull the hidden bundle until it lay sideways in its temporary lodging.

"Ah!" The muffled anguish scour the room. Her body convulsed in agony.

Liang wrapped her arm around her daughter's shoulder and whispered comfort into her ear. "You can do this, Jia-Li. Be brave. Only one more turn."

"Oh, Mama. I can't. I can't."

"You can, my darling. Please, you must try. Soon it will all be over, and you can rest. Ready?"

A muted sob escaped Jia-Li, and Liang nodded to Mary. The last push locked the baby into the proper birthing position as the exhausted young mother let out a horrific cry. Water gushed forth from her pelvis as the baby's amniotic sack broke.

"Now you can push, Jia-Li. Push!" Mary placed her hand near her pelvis. "I can feel the baby's head."

Samuel's face glowed with hope as he wiped Jia-Li's brow. "One more big push, my love. Our child wants to see his mother."

"Oh, Sam. I'm so tired. I'm trying."

"Liang, you may need to help her push. Place your hands on her stomach and press downward," Mary said.

Placing her hands on her daughter's abdomen, Liang pressured the dome-shaped mass as Jia-Li bore down with what little strength she had left.

The babe burst through his mother's gate, landing into Mary's welcoming hands. With the syringe, she suctioned the liquids from the baby's mouth. An instantaneous cry resounded from the slippery, pinkish, infant to announce his arrival.

"You have a son, Jia-Li and Samuel. A beautiful boy," Mary said, wiping him clean and laying him on his mother's chest.

Shaking with joy, Jia-Li and Samuel held their newborn child, and tears flowed. The extreme love between mother and child seemed to overcome all Jia-Li's pain and suffering.

"Welcome home, my son." Jia-Li whimpered. His mother's voice quieted the babe, and he opened his eyes to view her for the first time. An immediate bonding occurred as he relaxed into her arms. His dark hair resembled his father's, his dimples like his mother's, and his smile like an angel's.

"You have done well, my daughter and son," Mary said, "God's blessing is upon you and your new family."

Samuel stood and hugged both his mothers. "Thank you for all your help and being here in our time of need and great joy. You are part of His great blessings, and we are so grateful."

Liang swaddled a blanket about the infant. "Have you a name for your child?"

A wide grin of relief and overwhelming happiness spread across Samuel's face. "Yes, we've decided to name him Adam. Our firstborn."

22

Good News

The parlor shimmered from the tree's candlelight, and the aroma of the evening's feast still lingered after the family's hearty consumption. Immense felicity pulsed through Naomi as she took note of William's joyous participation in her family's festive holiday gaiety. The farmhouse filled with vibrant melodic carols. She strummed the dulcimer, her father plucked the banjo, Samuel swayed with the fiddle, Sarah tinkered on the mandolin, her mother harmonized sweet high notes. William interjected the melody on David's guitar. Lad, the children, Huang-Fu and Liang, clapped and sang along while baby Adam cooed in Jia-Li's arms.

Go tell it on the mountain,
Over the hills and everywhere,
Go tell it on the mountain,
Our Jesus Christ is born.

When I was a seeker
I sought both night and day,
I asked the Lord to help me,
And he showed me the way.

Go tell it on the mountain,
Over the hills and everywhere,
Go tell it on the mountain,
Our Jesus Christ is born.

He made me a watchman
Upon a city wall,
And if I am a Christian,
I am the least of all.

Go tell it on the mountain,
Over the hills and everywhere,
Go tell it on the mountain,
Our Jesus Christ is born.

Palms upon her chest, Mary tried to contain the overflowing adoration for her family, while sitting by the hearth beside her husband. "Oh my, only angels can orchestrate a greater strain. William, you did a mighty fine job playin' the guitar. Makes me pine for David. I do miss him so. I wished he and Clara were able to join us for Christmas. This is our second year without him, and I do love it when the entire family is together at this time."

Jonathan pat Mary's knee. "Only two more years until he returns home with his family."

Naomi's ears perked up, and a tinge of jealousy tried to emerge itself from deep within. However, she pushed it away and did her best to esteem her brother better than herself. "Family? Do tell, Pa."

"Oh, I guess I failed to mention with all the excitement of late. In David's most recent letter, he mentioned that Clara is with child."

Naomi gasped with gladness, as did the others. "Oh, good news indeed. But how is he going to support a family while attendin' college?"

"He's workin' part-time shoein' horses for his father-in-law at their livery stable on weekends. It's a good thing David and Clara are still residin' at her parent's home while he is still in school. It affords him the time to study instead of worryin' about how he is goin' to pay rent."

Samuel snickered. "Thank God for parents. We've all been in his shoes havin' to live under our parents' roof until we can stand on our own two feet. The weekends with his wife and family must be David's savin' grace after a strenuous week of study and livin' in the dormitory.

"Despite the horrifyin' experience I went through this summer, I count my blessin's. I have a beautiful wife and child, a lovin' family, a stable job, and a fine roof over my head."

"Here, here," Lad held up his glass of wine to toast in agreement.

Sarah gagged. "Brother dear, please allow me to interject my observation. Not all siblings have had to undergo such a humblin' experience. Our sweet sister, Naomi, never fretted a day in her secure life here on the farm."

Naomi huffed. "True, Pa and Ma assured the farm as my forever home if I remained a spinster the remainder of my life. Dear Sarah, allow me to correct you about my frettin'. Truth be told, I longed to find true love as y'all have ascertained, and the opportunity of raisin' my own family." She faced William. "I would, with good grace, give this all up to be with the one I love."

The room became still, and only the tick of the mantel clock chattered for a brief moment. William inhaled deep, and his countenance glowed from where he stood holding the guitar. He placed the musical instrument next to the couch as he viewed Naomi with abundant affection. All eyes watched as he moved toward her, where she sat. Kneeling before his beloved, he caressed her hands in his. "I believe this is the most opportune time to present my own good news."

He reached inside his coat pocket, expelled a small leather box, and pull open its cover to reveal a brilliantly shining diamond ring the size of a small marble. "Naomi, my dearest, I pray you will take my offer to secure your future under my roof, where I will provide for you and love you all the days of my life. Will you marry me?"

Naomi wrapped her arms around William's neck and kissed his face. "Oh, William, yes, I will marry you. I do believe my frettin' days are over."

The ambiance in the room set ablaze with applause as the family congratulated and embraced the newly engaged couple. When Mary's turn came to extend her well-wishes, she could only stutter, "But when? Where? What?" She positioned herself in front of William to get his undivided attention. "I thought you might be considerin' movin' to California."

William grimaced and searched for reassurance in Naomi's face. "Well, that is a decision I cannot make by myself. My wife will have some say in it too. Fifteen hundred acres of thriving corn land is a heritage worth considering.

"I hope to wed Naomi next week, take her on honeymoon to San Francisco and the Pacific Ocean, and immediately return home to Indiana with me. For now, a private wedding ceremony with family shall suffice. Someday soon after we settle down, I would like to plan a grand reception at my ..." he loosened his bow tie, "our farm perhaps in the spring. This will allow her time to become acquainted with her home in Indiana. After a year, we can reassess our choices and decide on the path which best suits us."

Warmth enveloped Naomi and peace, which surpasses understanding settled her soul. Her fearful thoughts of moving far from the home she ever knew collided with the commitment to be wed to the man who stole her heart on the dance floor at her brother's wedding. All anxiety dissipated because she trusted William, knowing he is God's choice for her. Both will pave the way in the new chapter of her life. "Your proposition is marvelous, darlin'. I'm in total agreement and look forward to discovering what awaits me in Indiana."

One glance at her mother's muted countenance rekindled a small spark of waver in Naomi. Homesickness did its best to overcome her gladness. No, get thee behind me, Satan! She quoted Matthew 16:23 in her mind. Ma will adjust as I will with the Lord's help. I refuse to allow any negative thoughts to cloud my happiness.

The sound of her father slapping his knee with approval and bellowing a grand hoop and holler affirm confidence for Naomi and Mary, which resulted in the women locking arms in agreement. He said with great satisfaction, "Well then, it's settled. I shall notify our pastor first thing tomorrow, and we shall plan a wedding ceremony on the first day of the New Year. It will be a new day, a new beginning, in a new home for the newlyweds!"

23

New Year New Life

Mid-morning on her wedding day, Naomi's heart swelled with grateful emotion as she examined her reflection in her parents' bedroom full-length mirror. "Oh, Ma, I'm so honored to be the recipient of your weddin' dress. You did well to pack it amongst the few items we were allowed to bring with us from Kentucky. I would've married in my best Sunday clothes, given the short amount of time to prepare. I never expected this!"

Being careful, Naomi twirled as she clutched the delicate faded white gathered lace of the simple country garment once embodied with hoops. She now wore her corset and corded petticoat beneath its fine folds. "Your wedding gown far exceeds my imaginations of selectin' a bridal ensemble. This is much more sentimental."

Restricted by the garment's snugness, she reached to hug the woman she most admired and adored. She envisioned her mother removing some stitches a few days earlier to fit her stocky physique better. Now she wore it with pride and great honor.

Mary tugged and adjusted the fabric as her eyes drip with liquid felicity. "I prayed this gown would breathe fresh air again and that I could pass it on to one of my daughters. Since Sarah eloped all my hopes rest with you, my darlin' girl."

Cupping Naomi's face in her palms, Mary kissed her forehead. "Yes, I had faith in our all-knowing Lord to choose a husband who can love you for everythin' you are. After all, it was He who said in Genesis 2:18, 'It is not good that the man should be alone; I will make him an help meet for him.' So I held God to his promises, and He was faithful to provide the perfect son-in-law your pa and I might ever pray for ... William."

Naomi beamed like a crystal goblet by a sunny window and sat at the dressing table mirror where her mother placed a sheet around her bodice in preparation of facial adornment. Laid out on a silver platter tray were a sundry of toiletries, cosmetics, and embellishments supplied by Sarah from the local apothecary. Never in her life did Naomi find a need to enhance her imagery. Eyes enlarged she could only stare at the array of bottles and round tins filled with balms and salves.

"Oh my, where do I begin?" Naomi said as she brushed over the tinctures.

"Don't you worry none. I'm no stranger to this application." Mary methodically reached for a small bottle filled with red liquid. "How else do you suppose I caught your father's eye at my sixteenth birthday party many moons ago?" she let out a sultry giggle.

Without effort, her mother began massaging Naomi's cheek with the red beet rouge, then dusted with her face with pearl powder, which helped to bring color and a silky white luster to her daughter's appearance. Next, she rubbed alkanet infused beeswax to the bride's lips to complement a rosy glow worthy of a kiss.

As her mother fuss over her, Naomi continued to share her thoughts. "My mind often ponders the path the Lord planned for me and William's chance encounter. Imagine, if David did not choose to attend college in Indiana, both my brother and I wouldn't have met our intended others. Had William and I not championed ourselves when the orchestra conductor called the single men and women at David's weddin', I'd be destined as a spinster at your heels, Ma.

"My fear is that I am beguiled by marital wanting. I do hope my decision to marry William is true. My heart tells me so, and I do look forward to some adventure beyond the Snelling boundaries with my forever companion. Who would've ever thought I would be the chick to leave the nest and fly away to another land?"

"Yes, however, the reason birds fly south is because they migrate to a warmer climate when winter sets in. Their instincts always bring them back home when spring arrives. I do pray you and William will return to us here in California, just as David and Clara will do when he finishes college. After all, we are now William's only surviving relatives by marital law."

"Indeed, they do, Ma. Let's pray your analogy applies to William and me."

Naomi reached for the milk color perfume bottle with hand-painted flowers. "I believe I am familiar with this added touch. I've always associated this beautiful lilac fragrance to you, Ma. It reminds me of those special occasions of you dressed in your finest." Upon opening the delicate container, the sweet floral bouquet filled the room, and Naomi dabbed behind her ears, wrist, and temples.

"And now for the final touch," Mary said as she pulled a drawer in her musical jewelry box. The tinker of pins striking a miniature rotating cylinder played Amazing Grace. There she found her pearl drop earrings worn on her wedding day and she fixed it on her daughter's ear lobes.

Too eager for the day to unfold, her mother's words skim her thoughts like a light dusting of snow moving with the wind.

A knock came, and Liang's voice filtered through the bedroom door. "Pastor McSwan and his family are here. Everyone is seated and waiting for you." Footsteps fade toward the stairs.

Mary pulled the thin veil over Naomi's floral crown and in front of her face. "All right, are you ready for your grand entrance, dear?"

Warmth filled Naomi's countenance. "Yes, Ma, more than I will ever be."

A ROUND BOUQUET of white and purple lupine amongst white narcissus accented the bride's attire as she and her mother glided down the staircase. At the parlor door, her father dressed in formal raiment awaited, eyes aglow by their arrival. My likeness to Ma on their weddin'

day thirty years ago must be in Pa's thoughts.

Her parents were the bedrock of her existence and moral upbringing. Their God-centered relationship will forever be the epitome of what wedlock should be. Dear Lord, I pray my marriage to William will conform to such a gracious standard.

"I thank you both for all you've done to raise and teach me about life. William chose me for who I am, and I accredit my stature to you. No human words can express how much love and respect I have for you."

A torrent of emotion enveloped them as they embraced. She kissed their faces and moved into position, resting her left hand over her father's. They waited in the foyer as her mother entered the room and took a seat. Drifting from the parlor, the Bridal March song played from Samuel's fiddle with gusto announcing their cue to enter.

Elation burst from within her as the transformed room came into view. Now a wedding hall, fronds of alabaster tulle and silken ribbon décor adorned its four walls. Samuel, Jia-Li, Sarah, Lad, the children, Ruth and Rebecca McSwan, Huang-Fu, Liang, Yung, Sheng-Li, Anguo, Patrick and Ingrid Fay, Mr. Jacobi, Marshal Warner, Dr. Cassidy, and Mr. Cavern. Except for David and Clara, they were all here to celebrate her momentous occasion. Memories flashed past her as she acknowledged her guest. They stood to shower her with rose petals as she walked among them toward the morning sunlight filtered through the lace curtains, which immersed her statuesque groom. The rays cast a brilliant shimmer upon her as she and her father marched inside.

The exchange took place from her father's hand into her betroths. An unusual calm enveloped her as she rested in his alluring masculine nature. The familiar scent of his cologne reminded her of the first time he held her on the dance floor. No strong cup of valerian tea can stop her knees from collapsing beneath her and slow her heart rate. However, William's manly bravado and sound assurance remedied all her fears. She could trust and rely upon this man who waited as long as she did for a soul mate. Now they were to be each other's forever companion under God's good graces.

The pastor began. "Dearly beloved. We are gathered here today to celebrate the wedding of William Tyne and Naomi Sower. This is a sacred and ancient right before Almighty God. For them, out of the routine of ordinary farming life, the extraordinary has happened. They met each other on the most unlikely of paths that span life's journey, fell in love, and are binding their relationship with their wedding. A good marriage must be created. Spouses are never too old to write love letters to one another, hold hands, enjoy a beautiful sunset together, and say 'I love you' every day. Matrimony is not just marrying the right person … it's being the right partner. There are no two people on this blessed earth who are more right for one another than this couple before me. No vast amount of land, mountains, deserts, or lakes can deter God's plans to bring them together. As Naomi and William prepare to join their lives, it is essential to understand that everyone present has and will continue to play a vital role in their future. Thus, we are here not only to witness their promises to each other but to bestow upon them our blessing. The couple will now read their vows."

Captured by William's amorous stag-like fixation on her and his massive rugged hands' warmth pressed against hers, a deep wanting for him bolster in her unlike she's ever felt before. Oh, dear God. I hope my carnality is hidden beneath this veil.

"I, Naomi, take thee, William, to be my wedded husband, to have and to hold, from this day forward, for better, for worse, for richer, for poorer, in sickness and in health, to love and to cherish, till death do us part, according to God's holy ordinance; and thereto I pledge thee myself to you."

The same vows were volleyed back to her by her husband-to-be.

"May I have the rings please?" said Pastor McSwan.

Little Billy, prodded forward by Sarah, balanced a pillow carrying two golden bands in his small arms.

"William, do you take Naomi to be your wife?"

"I do."

"Do you promise to love, honor, cherish and protect her, forsaking all others and holding only unto her?"

"I do."

"Naomi, do you take William to be your husband?"

"I do."

"Do you promise to love, honor, cherish and protect him, forsaking all others and holding only unto him?"

"I do."

The couple took turns placing the rings on each other's fingers and continued their vows. "This ring I give you is a symbol of my love. I pledge to share with you my heart, my home, and all my worldly goods, so help me, God."

"By the authority vested in me, I now pronounce you as husband and wife. You may now kiss your bride," Pastor McSwan said as William embraced her and encapsulated his lips upon Naomi's. The family applauded, and the pastor concluded the ceremony. "I present to you, Mr. and Mrs. William Tyne."

The family and friends exchanged congratulatory adulations. Amongst the gaiety, Jonathan said, "Please join us in the dining room for a celebratory luncheon." They gathered into the dining room as Huang-Fu, Liang, and additional kitchen staff served the meal.

Seated at the table, Naomi ruminated on the brilliant diamond, which graced her industrious hand. The dainty ring brought about an added sense of femininity to her indelicate nature. Her husband's hardy laughter promised a bright and happy future. Several trunks filled with her belongings awaited them in their wagon, and soon they would be boarding the stagecoach to San Francisco for their three-day honeymoon.

What she most longed for was to be on the train headed to Indiana so she could move forward into the new life, which piqued her curiosity six months anterior when she first met William Tyne in Indiana. The drastic change, long distance, lack of familiar faces and places lurked about her like dark, mysterious shadows in the night. But God's small still voice within her brought calm to her anxious spirit and spoke the words from Deuteronomy 31:6. 'Be strong and of a good courage, fear not, nor be afraid of them: for the LORD thy God, He it is that doth go with thee; He will not fail thee, nor forsake thee.'

24

Greensburg, Indiana

Naomi situated herself on a glossy wood bench shivering by another disembarked passenger at Greensburg's Big Four Train Station. The nervous paces of William's steps indicated apprehension as he peered out the window at the dense snowbanks in search of the horse and carriage driven by his head supervisor, Bert.

The expansive red-brick building with white trim hailed its established prominence in the assiduous town. Main lines of steam locomotives devoured and spewed passengers and never failed to cease its operations despite the deluge of windswept snow, adding another blanket to the frigid arctic-like landscape. The industrious expansion of Indiana's towns far exceeded California's growing communities because of the railroad. Is this the promise of the future the railroads proclaim? The hustle and bustle of travelers, streets lined with rows of two to three-story brick buildings, and churches the size of train depots overwhelmed her at a dizzying rate.

Good Lord, I miss California already. This town does not live up to its name Greensburg as everything is laden in white. This is a far cry from San Francisco's balmy winter temperature of 60 degrees. The thought of her and William tussling about on the down-filled comforter at the Palace Hotel's honeymoon suite brought warmth to her icicled extremities. And to think William's farmhouse required another 45 minutes of travel time in a carriage that might as well be a refrigerator train car.

"Ah ... there he is," William said and barked a command to her. "Wait there, dear, while I load our bags into the wagon. I'll fetch you when we are ready."

"Glad to oblige," she chuckled, trying to be cheerful over the miserable conditions.

One imagery amongst many that aided her to move back east was a warm, cozy farmhouse with a roaring hearth exhaling its breath of hot corn chowder and steamy cornbread cooking in cast iron crockery. They were almost home after almost two weeks of train travel, sleeping in the train's tight bunks and dining to its sway. She didn't complain, for this form of transportation surpassed the six-month relocation by ox driven covered wagons her family survived over ten years ago. She closed her eyes and imagined the warmth of a hot soothing bath.

"Your carriage awaits, Madame," William said with a phony English accent.

Naomi opened her eyes to have two pairs starring at her with smiles that could illuminate the entire room.

"Darlin', meet Bert. He is my head supervisor who oversees the sharecroppers at the farm." He turned to the lean six-foot middle-aged farmhand wearing a heavy wool-lined long coat and leather chaps. Small icicles hung from his mustache and beard like ornaments, and his eyebrows were covered in a layer of frost. His dark complexion contrast with the icy conglomeration which adorned him. "Bert, allow me to introduce my beautiful bride, Naomi."

"Please to meet ya, Mrs. Tyne," he said and tipped his snow-topped slouch hat.

"Likewise, Bert." She stood, curtsied then tightened her fur-lined paletot coat and bonnet.

"Several warm blankets to bundle up in are in the carriage. It's gonna be a cold ride home, I'm afraid." Bert shrugged his shoulders. "We best be goin'. Another blizzard is headed our way."

William lent his elbow. "Watch your step, dear. The snow is mighty deep."

She clutched his arm as they trod through the thick cold slush toward the carriage. The hem of her traveling skirt and her boot's soles were saturated. In the carriage's back seat, she and William layer the blankets on their laps and around their shoulders.

"Let's go home," William said. Bert waved the whip, and the horse jerked forward. Their warm breath turn to round balls of steam upon every exhale.

NOT ONE SIGN OF CORNFIELDS marked the acres of the flat landscape now cloaked in a sea of glistening white and engulfed by ominous clouds. In the distance, the two-story farmhouse's billowing puffs of chimney smoke and grey elevation crept closer to them like a lone grey wolf stocking its prey in a wintery tundra. Small bungalows with glowing windows where the sharecroppers live huddled near the barn, and they too had their chimneys roaring.

The carriage stopped in front of the house, which was the equivalent size to her parents' home in Snelling. It also had a handsome porch to the home's left side leading to the front door and bedecked with patio furniture and a cushioned porch swing for two. However, this home was covered in snow like ones depicted on Christmas cards.

"Welcome home, darlin'," William said with cheeks glowing red from the chilled air. He stepped out of the wagon and assisted her to the front porch. "Now, as tradition holds, I must carry you over the threshold. Are you ready?"

"Carry me?" She felt warmth rush to her cold face. "I've never been carried before in my entire life." Amused at the thought, hysterical laughter bolster forth from the newlyweds as William swoop her into his arms. "Oh! Don't hurt yourself, my love."

Bert sprang forward, opened the front door, and allowed the jubilant pair to enter. Packed luggage in his arms, he carried them upstairs to the master bedroom.

Inside the foyer, William placed Naomi on her feet. "Let me get your coat, dear."

Like a child in a toy store, Naomi's eyes were astounded by the homes welcoming interior and homey décor. A handwoven rug grace the front entrance, on the wall were several dowels to hang winter coats, and on the floor a wrought iron basket for umbrellas. Atop a long table in the hallway, a collection of tintype pictures, pottery, and framed embroidery display some of the Tyne family relicts. The Warmth from the parlor's crackling fireplace found its way to Naomi and touched her face, her hands as she removed her knit gloves, and her entire being.

The aroma of a warm meal drew her sights to the room to the right where pots and pans clattered, and an elder heavy set Negro woman prepared supper in the broad and long kitchen while humming a song. She let out a hearty cackle to hear William's voice. Wiping her hands on her apron, she seemed to bounce upon her approach toward them. Her wide grin revealed white shining teeth against her dark chocolate colored features. Thick arms wrap around his neck as she gave William a grand bear hug. "Mr. Tyne, your home!"

"Naomi, meet Etta. She has been with my family since I was a wee boy. She chose to stay and be in my employ. I don't know if I could ever do without her."

"Hello, Etta. You have me spellbound. Somethin' smells divine comin' from that kitchen." Naomi craned her neck and lifted her nose to inhale the aroma of chicken pot pie and cornbread cooking in the oven.

"So pleased to meet ya too, Mrs. Tyne. When Mr. Tyne tolls us he was afetchin' hims a wife, the entire house staff went straight away to prepare for your arrival. I'm sure ya both are starvin'. Y'all settle in, and supper will be ready shortly."

"Come, dear, let me give you a quick tour of our home." William guided her to the family room, which beckoned their presence with its country charm. More tintypes of family and acquaintances perched on the dual hearth's mantel, which also warmed his adjacent office. A harp-shaped dulcimer sat strategically in the room's center. With the spoon like hammer, Naomi tapped on a couple of strings as its bright and magical sound resonate.

"My family too was quite musical," William said, following close behind her. "Many evenings were spent with my parents and siblings entertaining ourselves with songs brought down through our lineage.

Now that my parents are gone, and my sisters are married, the gaiety has been suppressed for another time. And I do hope that time has arrived." His eyes glistened, and his words choked as he reminisced.

"Oh, my darlin', William, together we shall fill this home with so much love, music, laughter, and children to our heart's content. That time is now."

"Well then, my wife, with that said shall we get started on those plans right away. Shall we remove these wet garments, soak in a hot tub, and make our contentment. This way, please." He pointed upstairs to the bedrooms, took her by the hand, and without restraint, she followed.

Oh, my beloved husband, I do hope I can give you children. Otherwise, this will be a dreary, lonely home. I pray I can be a good wife and mother, and carry on the Tyne legacy for William's sake. If only I had family close by when it comes time to bring our babes into this world, especially Ma. Naomi shiver at the thought of herself giving birth with a doctor or midwife unbeknownst to her by her side. Sadness and heartache tried to distract her, so she pushed the imagery aside and dwelt on the nearest relative instead. David and Clara must come and visit when winter is passed. Visions of them and their children came to mind, which led back to her husband, William, and their home. In the meantime, I must find somethin' to do to stay busy and keep from goin' stir crazy. Oh, Lord, help me.

25

His Test

Frantic students darted from one classroom to the next oblivious to the sun's heat and the muggy humidity which surrounded them. The tension drew heavy on campus as only two weeks remained of the school season, and the looming finals congested the ambitious undergraduates' lives. Book ladened carpetbag in hand, David trudged into the stately red brick building, to his classroom and found his claimed seat for the past six months. The professor scribbled the day's lesson on the chalkboard as his classmates piled inside chattering about subjects. The students hushed and the lecture began as active pens scratched upon paper.

Halfway through the session, several heads, including himself, turned around distracted by the creaking sound of the classroom's back door opening. An administrative aide slid into the classroom, doing his best to be discreet and not interrupt the instructor. He whispered in the ear of the first student seated closest to the door, who then points David's way.

The man slunk toward him with a note in his hand. He bent and murmured, "Are you David Sower?"

"Yes."

"An urgent telegraph came for you." He placed the folded paper on David's desk, and as stealthy he entered, he exited in the same manner.

The message read, You will soon be a father. Clara's in labor.

Elated and confused, David's focus on the professor failed him as the imagery of his wife delivering their child without him troubled his thoughts. The baby is early. It's not due until the end of June after this semester. What am I to do, Lord? Should I pack my things and leave now to be by her side or stay? The next few days' lessons are crucial for next week's finals. If I depart now, I can hop on the train, be home for my child's birth, and return early the next morning. Ah, but I will miss my morning courses, and I need the time to study. If only her labor occurred on my usual weekend recrudescence.

He huffed at his senseless and ludicrous deduce when the most trying dilemma perturbed him. Are you testing me, Lord? Do You want to know where my loyalties lay?

Jesus' words came to him strong and clear from Mark 12:30-31, And thou shalt love the Lord thy God with all thy heart, and with all thy soul, and with all thy mind, and with all thy strength: this is the first commandment.

And the second is like, namely this, Thou shalt love thy neighbor as thyself. There is none other commandment greater than these.

Heart immerse in anguish, David realized what he must do. He had to stay focused on the course set before him. Clara understands this. Besides, she has her family by her side to assist her. No matter how much he reasoned with himself, the guilt of not being there when his wife needed him most pounded at him like a blacksmith's hammer. All he could do now is close his eyes and send a prayer.

Oh, heavenly Father, I thank You for Your goodness and blessings upon my life. Especially for my wife and child, who is soon to come into this world. Please, Lord, be with them at this unexpected time of labor. I put my trust in You to give Clara strength and deliver our babe safe. Although I love them so very much, they are second to You. Shower her and her family with understanding for my temporary absence as I consider You first in all I do. Thank You, Lord. Amen.

"Is there a problem, Mr. Sower?" The professor asked as all eyes were upon him.

"Uh, oh no, sir. All is well. I'm soon to be a father." He took a deep breath as the class responded with good wishes.

The gracious pepper haired instructor tapped on his desk and quoted Psalm 127:5a, "Happy is the man that hath his quiver full of them; he shall not be ashamed. Congratulations, young gent. Let us continue with our lessons, students."

A calming peace fell upon David as he refocused himself. Clara and our babe are in the Lord's merciful care. I will send a telegram to them when this class is over.

A GLIMMER OF LIGHT crept over the horizon foretelling the dawns awake as David and his brother-in-law, Clarence, stepped off the train then waited in Marion's station. He peered at his timepiece as Clayton Harrington arrived on time as usual with the wagon to fetch them. From there, their usual destination would bring them to his in-law's home for a hasty greeting with his wife, then off to the family's blacksmith shop to shoe horses. However, today's schedule bent.

He searched Clayton's facial expression for any sign of disappointment in him for not arriving a few days earlier to assist in Clara's most trying hour. Nothing. Instead, his father-in-law's tender compassion prevailed.

"Congratulations, son! I'm sure you are anxious to get home to see your wife and child."

Clarence chuckled. "That's all he could think and talk about the last couple of days. He was like a rope being tugged at from both ends. But alas, the Lord won that fight. I'm sure if circumstances were different and you and mother were not nearby, he would've dropped what he was doing and been here lickety-split."

"You have that right, Clarence," David said. "Yes, father, I've been a wreck and had every intention to be here for our child's birth. That was me and Clara's plan based on the baby's due date. We were confident of its end of June arrival and didn't make any allowance for deviation in the schedule. You must think me the most wretched of husbands for the decision I made. For that, I am ashamed."

Slouched in his seat, David shuffled his feet and kicked his carpetbag of books. "I did pray every moment I was able for Clara and the baby's safe delivery. I hope all went well."

Clayton elbowed David as if waking a drunkard from slumber. "Yes. She came through fine. Don't beat yourself up, son. Clara knew what she was getting herself into when she married you. We all did. The Lord's calling comes first in your life, and you must be obedient to Him."

The horse's reins snapped as Clayton hastened its trot while quoting Proverbs 16:9. "'A man's heart deviseth his way: but the LORD directeth his steps.' The Lord is in control of all situations, and we had to trust that He had a reason for allowing your little one to arrive early during an austere time in your life. I believe your decision to stay on course is pleasing to the Lord. Clara understands that, and so do we. There lay your strength. For that, you will reap a reward. Come on, son, cheer up. You have just joined the ranks of fatherhood!"

The gloom lifted, and David sat erect. "Thank you, father, for the words of encouragement. I needed to hear that from you." He rubbed the heaviness from his neck. "And how is the baby doing being premature?"

"The babe is a wee small, but proper nurturing should remedy that." Clayton gag. "All right, I say no more. I know what your next question will be. I don't want to ruin the surprise. I'll reserve that special moment for you and your wife."

With that said, David pried no more. His father-in-law would not divulge any more pertinent information. Instead, they discussed business matters at the shop. He will have to discover for himself whether he has a son or daughter and of his wife's condition. The day likened itself to the anticipation of a birthday party, with all its jubilant activities and veiled gifts waiting to be unwrapped by the celebrant. The expectancy brought David interim relief from the head-numbing bombardment of collegiate education. He looked forward to the summer break to spend time with his family.

THE BEDROOM WINDOW sunlight sprayed a luminous aura upon the nursing mother and her babe reclining on their bed. The bouquet of fresh flowers he ordered for her, which accompanied his telegram a few days ago, sat on their dresser. The room's cheerful brightness and his wife's glowing countenance posed no inclination of difficulty she encountered while giving birth. When she glanced his way, her gentile smile permitted his entrance as the others stayed behind, allowing the new family privacy. David removed his hat, tiptoed inside, knelt at their bedside, and kiss Clara's cheek.

"Meet your son," she said.

Joy welled in his soul. "Hello, my handsome fellow." David caressed his pinkish face as he suckled on his mama's breast. "You look radiant, Clara, dear. Father tells me all went well. How I wished I could've been here with you. I'm so very sorry."

Clara squeezed David's hand. "Oh darlin', no need to apologize. I understand. I agonized about whether to tell you knowing how difficult it is for you at this time. But I also knew that you would not forgive me had I remained silent about our good news."

"Have you chosen him a name?"

"No, I haven't. I'll leave that task up to you. My part is done." She giggled, and the babe let go, opened his eyes, peered into David's, and let out a content coo as if he recognized his father's voice.

David chortle. "Your name shall be Isaac since you have brought laughter to your mother and me."

Clara gasp. "That's a perfect name. Isaac, he shall be. Would you like to hold him?"

"Of course."

The swaddled wee infant lay in David's arms as they sway on the rocking chair beside the bed. Thank you, Lord, for this precious gift. Love created this, and he is mine. The peaceful moment and rhythmic motion rekindle a lullaby his mother used to sing to him as a babe. So the young father sang in a low, soothing voice Sleep, Baby, Sleep.

Sleep, baby, sleep
Your father tends the sheep
Your mother shakes the dreamland tree
And from it fall sweet dreams for thee
Sleep, baby, sleep

Sleep, baby, sleep
Sleep, baby, sleep
Our cottage vale is deep
The little lamb is on the green
With snowy fleece so soft and clean
Sleep, baby, sleep
Sleep, baby, sleep

26

Reception

The humidity caused the corn to grow taller than a farmer. Green symmetrical rows now circumferenced the farmhouse and barn where snow blanketed the land only eight months earlier. The sultry farmhouse's grounds made for a lovely country wedding reception decorated with a few linen-covered tables which tout floral centerpieces of wild blue indigo, purple coneflower, and claret lobelia. A mowed lawn designated the dance floor area next to the four-piece country bluegrass band. Naomi could not contain her heart's gladness as their guest reciprocated smiles brighter than the dazzling daylight illuminating the countryside.

Standing at the head table with William, Naomi clung to his elbow and addressed their guest. "We're grateful y'all can come durin' Indiana's brutal summer months. We did our best to schedule the reception at a time most appropriate for all after Isaac's birth and before harvest and the fall college semester begins."

Naomi squeezed her husband's arm a little tighter. "I thought this day would never arrive. I shall enjoy the next two weeks of recreation with the family at our farm. Your absence in my life causes my heart's fondness to swell. I thank God for my lovin' and supportive husband. Without his strength and encouragement, I don't know how I would've survived the Indiana winter. Alas, spring and summer arrived as he promised. I do believe I'm beginnin' to enjoy Indiana's four seasons."

William pressed a kiss on Naomi's brow then address their guest. "Yes, folks, I'm going to make Naomi a Hoosier yet! Welcome to our nest. One day she and I hope to fill this noble farm with many Hoosieroons. John Finley described them as having mush-and-milk, tin-cups, spoons, white heads, bare feet, and dirty faces who live and work in fields widening by stealth and increasing wealth."

William's face radiate as he patted Naomi's hand. "Farmin' corn is my entire life, and I must say with Naomi by my side, she ignites new meaning and purpose to my rudimentary existence. Her presence is like a cool breeze on a hot summer day," he laughed, "like today. Without further ado, please make yourselves at home, help yourselves to the buffet's bounty, and let's get this country shin-dig goin'."

William waved to the band, and the folk music began comprised of fiddle, banjo, guitar, and mandolin. Soon their guest found themselves kicking up their heels to the live music as the newlywed couple made their rounds visiting with family and friends.

AS WILLIAM AND JONATHAN WALK THE GROUNDS and her children, except for Naomi, chase their own on the lawn and gloated over their growing families, Mary took the opportunity to chat with her once headstrong and vivacious daughter. Beneath Naomi's smiles and cheering disposition, Mary detected a suppressed gloominess in the young lady that needed to be addressed and remedied. Her daughter's ambivalent stare at her siblings and their children ached of wanting and loneliness.

Mary recognized this familiar pining that once troubled her soul when she and Jonathan moved out west away from all familiar surroundings and relationships in Kentucky. The difference is she had the companionship of her adventurous brood, which kept her occupied and prohibited the ill emotion from festering. She was fully aware that creature comforts afforded on a remote yet successful farm would not suffice any woman's need to be surrounded by those she loves.

"Have you met any of your neighbors yet?" Mary asked.

Naomi jerked and reeled in her attention as if startled by Mary's astuteness. "Uh," she fidgeted with the glass on her lap. "Oh, no, not yet, Ma. The nearest neighbor is about five miles from here, and the town is almost an hour away."

"So, what do you do for social interaction?"

"Well," Naomi gulp some tea. "I, I talk to the cows and chickens and, on occasion, pester Etta in the kitchen, when she lets me."

"And William ... what does he do?"

"Oh, Ma, you know well enough how the farmin' chores keep our men busy. He operates this farm like a well-oiled machine. William is allowin' time for me to adjust to my new life before permittin' me to manage the accountin' ledgers. I believe he is waitin' until I've experienced a full harvest season. The sharecroppers and staff maintain the daily tasks, and frankly, nothin' is left for me to do. Embroidery and knittin' are my constant companion."

"A real lady of leisure," Mary said, trying not to sound too sarcastic. "Well, little ones shall keep you plenty busy."

Hidden grievances spew from Naomi's breath like corn popping in hot oil while she turned her back to hide her distraught composure. "What if that never happens, Ma? Eight months have come and gone, and I'm still without a child.

"With no friends or family, and not even a church I can attend with regularity, I'm goin' stir crazy. Had we been a little closer to town, I'd find other social activities. I love William, but the majority of the time, he is consumed by exhausting farm chores. And upon his return, any chance of romance escapes him."

Naomi turned to face her. "I'm miserable, Ma. As much as I appreciate the plenitude here, I want to go back home to Snelling."

Mary held her breath and measured her words of encouragement as she held her daughter's hand. "Do you remember last year when you cried to me because you feared you would never marry? Do you recall my suggestion?"

Pausing to reflect, Naomi shrugged her shoulders. "Yes, I do. You told me to keep knocking on God's door and badger Him with my constant plea." She gritted her teeth. "That's my first prayer every time

I'm alone. God is ignorin' me!"

"Well, He hasn't said 'no' either. God's perfect timin' requires patience, dear. Your good health and stature in life is an indication of His blessings toward you."

"He has endowed every gift except for what matters most. A family."

"What matters most is that your God and Father's foreknowledge is instrumental in decidin' what is best for you. Perhaps that is God's lesson for you to love and trust Him alone and be content with His will for you. For me, that revelation came when we near died in the desert from heat and starvation when comin' out to California."

Scanning each of her family members on the lawn as they clogged to the music, she cringed at the thought of that difficult moment. "While all of you withered, the thought occurred to me, 'If I were the only one to survive and lose everythin', would I continue to love and trust the Lord? Or would I be bitter and blame Him for allowin' my family to die?"

She locked her focus on Naomi. "Sound familiar? It should because this is what the Israelites did when they followed Moses into the desert to get to the Promise Land and encountered difficulties along the way. They grumbled, complained, and doubted God despite all the miracles He performed."

Naomi rolled up her shirtsleeves to cool from the heat of the subject and the day. "Yes, ma, that is a memory I would soon like to forget."

"Who was I to despise God's decision if he had a change of mind in our family's destination and desired us to entire Paradise instead of California? After all, He is God, the ultimate authority over all creation. I had to trust, accept, and be contented with His choice no matter what the outcome because He chose the best path for me based on His foreknowledge of things to come."

Naomi scratched her temple. "Oh, I never thought of it in that way. Gosh, why should we bother makin' our requests to Him if a plan is already in motion?"

"That's just it. Our requests trigger God's resolve. What's most amazing is that He is aware of what we are going to ask of Him and has an answer, whether it be 'yes,' 'no,' or 'later.' He revealed His plans for our family when your father and I asked Him for direction to our disparaging situation while living at the war-torn Kentucky farm. We knew we needed to move … but where? We wanted this place to be according to His will."

Again, Mary scoured her memory for the time she and Jonathan attended the Perryville church seeking God for their troubled lives. "His answer came in a vision, confirmed with scripture, and initiated by circumstances which guided us to the correct path. This plan was the sole reason why we moved in the first place."

Mary's thoughts returned to the desert experience. "With that destiny in mind, I held God to His resolution. He came through that fateful day and provided us nourishment with the death of one of the oxen. It was a worthy sacrifice to save us all. Just like what Jesus did for those who choose to believe in Him."

"So are you sayin' that I should continue to love and trust God no matter what His decision is for me because He knows best whether I should bear children or not?"

"Yes, just like Apostle Paul when he said he learned in whatever state he was in, to be content: how to be abased, and how to abound. Everywhere and in all things, he experienced fulfillment both to be full and to be hungry, both abundance and to suffer need. He was able to do all things through Christ who strengthened him."

Mary sipped on a glass of sweet tea then wiped the sweat from her forehead. "You must learn to do the same, whether you conceive or not. Without a doubt, your lovin' husband would do as you request even if it means sellin' this property and movin' to California. I do believe God gave him a vision of a fertile wife and numerous children on a farm. The question is, 'will this farm be in Indiana or California?' You need to hold God to that promise. However," she paused and inhaled deep, "be bendable should He decide a different path."

She squeezed Naomi's hand. "God did a mighty work bringin' the both of you together from faraway lands. A purpose is laid out for you, dear. Cling to that thought." She chuckled. "But once again, it doesn't hurt to plead your case to God as the widow did with the unjust judge I mentioned to you last year. The Bible tells of Sarah and Hannah doin' the same when they so wanted a child. Keep knockin' on God's door, darlin', and never stop lovin' and trustin' Him no matter what."

The gloom lifted from Naomi's countenance like the San Joaquin Tule fog dissipating from the sun's bolstering light bringing clarity far and wide. They joined the family on the dance floor and celebrated the Lord's bountiful blessings upon all of them.

Dear Lord, I do pray for my daughter's happiness. Please fill their home with your promise of children.

27

Do Not Be Afraid

June 1878

As the stagecoach wheels rolled through his boyhood town, childhood reflections scattered in David's thoughts. Four years of college scarce diminished the longing David had in his heart to preach the Gospel to the Chinese in his hometown, Snelling. This monumental step behind him, he can now proceed on his calling at home with his wife and son beside him. Clara, two-year-old Isaac, and the other passengers peered out the window as eager to settle down after ten days of steam locomotive and stagecoach travel.

"To your left on Green Street is the red brick church where your pa gave his first sermon," David said as he pointed outside while holding his toddler on his lap.

As they turned on the road called Lewis, he strained his neck to the west. "Darlin', the Chinese camp is on the other end of town."

Travel weary, Clara pushed a graceful smile.

"Ah, Jacobi's Mercantile. I purchased many sweets in that shop. I must take you there, son." He cast his sight across the road. "The white two-story building is the Snelling Courthouse where Pastor McSwan held our church's first gatherings. Further down is the grade school

I attended. Then less than a mile afterward is my family's farm. So we are almost home, my dear ones."

The stagecoach came to a stop, and all on board disembarked. Waiting at the depot were his parents with grins as bright as the early summer sunshine.

"So glad you are home, son." Jonathan wrapped his arms around David's shoulders.

"Welcome to California, Clara, and Isaac," Mary said as she embraced her daughter-in-law and grandson, who stood at his mother's skirt. "Y'all must be hungry and exhausted. Our carriage is across the street, and home is another fifteen minutes away."

"We are, but I desire to stretch my legs after being caged like an animal on the train and stagecoach. I look forward to strolling along the wayside path beside the wheat fields and then reclining on the front porch with a glass of cool lemonade. David has told me so much about Sower Farm that I feel I've always belonged here. That is until we can find a place of our own." Clara snickered as her husband and father-in-law procured their luggage.

"Well, we have plenty of room, and there is no rush to vacate. Our farm is your home now, and you are welcome to stay as long as you like." Mary scooped Isaac into her arms as they headed toward the carriage.

Everyone seated, Jonathan flicked the rein, and the horse pulled into a steady trot. "I hope you both don't mind, but we've invited the McSwans over for supper a few days from now. They are most eager to visit with you again, son, and your family."

David glanced at his spouse, who reciprocated a nod. "I'm anxious as well to introduce Clara and Isaac to Pastor Daniel and Ruth. They'll be happy to see I've returned fully equipped for the ministry with Bible wisdom, knowledge, and a supportive and gifted wife to boot."

"Indeed. The good Lord has prepared you well. All you need now is the opportunity to put all that training into good use."

"That time will surely come soon enough, Pa." David laughed.

CLARA'S EYES GREW LARGER THAN HEN'S EGGS as the carriage pulled through the wayside path toward the Sower farmhouse. The mature wheat fields moved with the balmy summer breeze, and the farmhands busied about their chores. Never had she seen so many Asian workers. They chattered amongst one another in an unfamiliar language expelling sharp, articulate pronunciation as if to a cadence. As her father-in-law stopped the carriage in front of their home, a man in a frog jacket, dark cap, and a long pepper colored queue, and a younger man dressed similarly greeted them.

"Welcome home, Mr. David and Mrs. Clara." The elder man bow. "This must be young Isaac." He patted the toddler's head situated in her arms. "I am Huang-Fu, the butler, and this is the house-boy, Ah Teny. Let us know how we can serve you." He turned to his counterpart. "Quick. Take their luggage upstairs to Mr. David's bedroom."

Clara curtsied. "Pleased to meet you."

Her husband extended the senior a hearty handshake. "Good to be back, my friend."

"Your room is ready, Mr. David. Liang has prepared lunch. I am happy to draw the bath for you and your wife later this evening," Huang-Fu said.

"Ah, yes. That would be most appreciated." David placed his hand on the small of her back. The gentle pressure indicated his eagerness to follow his parents into the home so they might settle in. "Darlin', let's change out of these travel apparel."

The spacious farmhouse lavished compared to the simple suburban home of her youth. She never had house staff at her beckoning call. "Oh my, husband, I shall be spoiled here."

TWO DAYS LATER, the summer calefaction beckoned the Sowers and their guest, Daniel and Ruth, to leisure and dine under the cool shade of the grand oak tree beside the farmhouse. The employees assembled a long table with a checkered table covering and a vase of yellow and purple daisies beneath the trees wide-reaching canopy. As the family relaxed, Liang, Huang-Fu, and Ah Teny served platters of exquisite stir-fried cuisine and refreshing lemon tea. The setting sun's rays trickled through the branches and cast a warm golden aura upon everyone and their surroundings.

David wiped his mouth and placed his napkin on the table. "Delicious supper, Liang. I've missed your delicious fine cooking."

"Thank you, sir. I prepare special meal for you, your family, and our guest. Hope soon we begin Bible lessons again." The graying haired woman in a simple Chinese frog shirt and skirt move forward with Ah Teny as he began to bus the table.

Leaning back in her chair, Clara exhaled and rubbed her belly with delight. "Now, I understand why my husband has a clear calling to the Chinese. Not only is their cuisine divine, but they are the most humble and hardworking people."

Jonathan lit his pipe as puffs of smoke pass his lips along with short bursts of cough. Then in nonchalant fashion, he pressed on his shoulder where his old war wound lay. "You've perceived them well, Clara. We prefer our Asian staff and employees above all others for their defining qualities."

A grunt escaped Daniel McSwan. "I'm ashamed to say; not all share the same sentiments toward the Chinese as we do. The majority of Californians are imposing more sanctions against their immigration to the United States and their employment. Many of these immigrants are considering the return to their homeland as other peoples are making life miserable for them on American soil."

Ruth sat erect. "Very few attend our services and sit at the back of the church. The tensions between them and our white parishioners do not go unnoticed even in the Lord's house. Very unsettling indeed and most grievous to the Holy Spirit."

Holding his wife's hand as if to steady her emotions, Daniel focused on David and Clara. "The need for a church dedicated to our Asian brethren would curtail this dilemma. The majority of these immigrants reside in a town of their own about three hours north of Snelling appropriately named Chinese Camp. One day our hope is for the Lord to open a door of opportunity to bring the Gospel to this place and establish His church."

David seemed to read Clara's discomfort with the perspective vision as she shifted in her seat. Scripture is what she needs to calm her fears. "Jesus tells us in Acts 1:8, 'But ye shall receive power, after that the Holy Ghost is come upon you: and ye shall be witnesses unto me both in Jerusalem, and in all Judaea, and in Samaria, and unto the uttermost part of the earth.'"

Sweat from her palms trickled between his hand and hers. "Darlin', we shall witness to them first here in Snelling, our Jerusalem. Then move outwards to Chinese Camp and maybe even one day to China itself." He grinned. "The uttermost part of the earth."

Clara's face flushed its rosiness, and she tightened her grip into his. "To China. My, my, husband that is quite ambitious."

"Do not be afraid, my dear. The Lord will not give us more than we can handle. Who knows? Perhaps He will raise one amongst the indigenous to send out to their countrymen. I may only be the Lord's instrument to teach and train up this individual. I hope to provide services here in Snelling's Chinese camp so that these brethren can worship the Lord without prejudice's prohibition."

His wife's body relaxed, and her grip loosened. The rosy color returned to her cheeks. "Ah, this vision is clearer to me and has my agreement."

Felicity rebound within David, which confirmed his mission's direction. Aware of the staff's attentive reactions toward the subject as they gathered close to the table, David raised his glass. "Well, here is to those of our household and community whom we can appreciate as fellow human beings first before ethnicity. They are in need of a Savior as we all do." He addressed Liang. "Yes, Liang and Huang-Fu, we shall resume our lessons, and I hope we together can reach many more of your countrymen with the Gospel of Jesus Christ."

After the family and their guest toast, Jonathan stood. "Shall we go to the parlor and continue our acquaintances. Please feel free to join us Huang-Fu and Liang."

The aging butler bow. "The honor will be ours, Mr. Jonathan."

28

Save Me, O God

"Etta, must you go too? I do enjoy your company," Naomi said as she placed the breakfast plates in the bin, and the robust Negro cook washed the dishes. William scarfed the remains of his morning meal, stood by the window as he gulped the last drop of coffee, and viewed the workers outside. Harvest time always added increased commotion among his employees. Large empty baskets stacked high on the wagon beds await their filling of fresh-cut corn. Bert's arms wave in every direction as he barked his commands to the farmhands.

"You know I must, Ms. Naomi. All hands are needed for the harvest. Not to worry, though. I'll be home before the others to prepare us supper. I've made you and the mister some pork sandwiches for lunch. Yours be sittin' on the counter wrapped in that brown paper, and Mr. William yours is in your basket as usual." The cheerful woman roamed about in the kitchen humming Spiritual songs. "Besides, I enjoy bein' outdoors in this marvelous sunshine."

Naomi stood beside her husband and placed her hand on his forearm to assert a suggestion. "Perhaps I can join all of you."

William returned a stern brow, and aggressive head shaking. "No, dear. The cornfield is no place for my lovely wife. You know that. It's not like the waist-high wheat, where you can be vigilant with the activity about you. You never know what may be lurking around the tall corn stalks. Not only are there snakes and wild creatures, but the men are starved for a woman's touch in these remote parts."

Removing her kitchen apron to don a loose tattered overdress, Etta wagged her finger. "Yes, ma'am. I work close by my husband and carries with me a sharp sickle for protection. There be occasions when I've been propositioned by one of them hooligans. One wave of this weapon, and they leave me be." She snarl, eyes wide open. "When menfolk are desperate, they can get all kinds of ideas in their fool heads. You best be at home, misses. I'll be sure to bring us back some fresh corn for dinner."

Naomi huffed perturb at her situation. Etta's spiel spurred another idea in her apprehensive mind. Locking her attention on her husband, she urged, "I can stay by you, dear."

William pulled away from her clutch and marched back to the kitchen table to gather his belongings. "I'm not always there to pick the corn. I've to manage these men, and that is not a sight you'll want to see. Some of them can be as stubborn as mules." He placed his straw hat on his head and stomped toward the front door.

Disappointed, Naomi scurried behind her husband and Etta. On the front porch, William turned to her as Etta joined the others. She hesitated, but she kissed his cheek and waved him off to the work field, her daily routine for the past two years of marriage.

The sinking heartache of confinement with nothing but her menial projects troubled her. Should she dare to capitulate to a rebellious nature by disobeying her husband's orders and file in with the workers? No. Don't go there, Naomi.

The words of Jesus rebuking his disciple Peter because of his defiance rang clear. Get thee behind me, Satan: thou art an offense unto me: for thou savourest not the things that be of God, but those that be of men. Her flesh cried out to subdue the loneliness, which subjugated her. She clung to Psalm 27:14 as her saving grace. 'Wait on the Lord: be of good courage, and He shall strengthen thine heart: wait, I say, on the Lord.'

What shall I do today? She turned and trudged into the parlor where her needlework lay waiting by her chair. She pawed at the lengthy tapestry almost completed. Involuntary tears well in her eyes and droplets pelt the frivolous artwork causing her to realize how deep her misery indwelled her.

She collapsed on the chair and wept aloud, aware of her solitude. David's words in Psalm 69 bereaved her emotions. 'Save me, O God; for the waters are come in unto my soul. I sink in deep mire, where there is no standing: I am come into deep waters, where the floods overflow me. I am weary of my crying: my throat is dried: mine eyes fail while I wait for my God.'

Alone and barren. Naomi's thoughts, the sound of her breathing, and the clock's ticking day after day chipped away at her sanity. No children to keep her happy, busy, and purposeful. At least for a time, she had her nephew Isaac and his parents to visit on occasion to break up the monotony. Oh, David, Clara, and Isaac, I wished you had stayed in Indiana. What will I do without any kin nearby to visit? They were gone and returned to the happy home she so longed for in Snelling.

Envy and frustration intensify, and she cried out. "Lord, if you will not grant me children, then I'm better off returning home to my parents where I can be more useful. I cannot stand another lonely moment in this destitute place. All the material contentment does not measure to the reciprocated love of family and friends. That's what is important to me. Not all this." She wiped her eyes and breathed deeply as she scanned the well-endowed parlor.

Her heart near stopped when her attention drew to her husband, who stood stunned at the parlor entrance. How long had he been standing there?

"I forgot my work gloves and came back to retrieve them when I heard you crying," he said. Traipsing toward his wife, he dropped to his knees at her feet.

"Oh, my William. I'm so sorry you heard that." Her emotions liquefy, and she burst into uncontrollable shaking. He wrapped his arms around her as if to restrain the convulsions.

"Now, now. No need to apologize. Often I've wondered how you were fairing but have been afraid to ask. And now, I know. I should be the one to ask for your forgiveness. I brought you here away from all those you love. This solitary hard life is all I've ever known, and I guess I've become accustomed to it. It's kept me busy. But you …"

he caressed her head and pressed it against his chest "... how insensitive of me. What can I do to make you happy, my love?"

"Don't get me wrong, my husband. You do make me happy. I love you with all my heart. However, I fear I've failed you by my infertility. I'm good for nothin' but another mouth to feed. Perhaps I'm not the wife you envisioned who'll provide you with a home full of children. Everyone in this household has a duty to fill, and mine was to be a mother. But how can I without little ones to tend to? At least your employees have a purpose. There is nothin' left in this place for me to put my hands on. Please, if you desire to send me back to my family, then I will understand."

William pushed back and peered into her soul. "You speak as if I were a cattleman with the sole purpose to breed and prosper. That isn't so. I love you too, Naomi, and you are more precious to me than rubies. I don't wish to send you away. I'll be patient and wait on the Lord. He brought us together for a reason, and I'll hold onto His promise. In the meantime, I realize boredom has overtaken you. I believe it's time you manage the accounting of this corn business, and first thing next week, we shall begin your training on my ledgers."

Naomi responded with a slow nod and a peakish grin. Isn't this what she was hoping for? Work, to be purposed. So why wasn't she exuberant at his premise? Without thinking, her gaze settled upon her barren anatomy and idle hands.

William lifted her chin. "I also know you've been lonely. What would you say if we visit your family after the harvest and stay till the next planting season? We can do this every year until we have a family of our own."

Without hesitation, her arms flew around his neck. This proposal sparked excitement in her and pushed out any ounce of gloominess. She longed to be with family, friends, familiar faces, and places. "Oh, William, you have made me a happy woman indeed. I would truly love to do that."

He then responded in the same manner as she did, lacking exuberance.

Her heart tore because she loved her husband beyond words and yet understood his deep sentiments toward his farm. The possibility of selling his family inheritance and moving to California must be lingering in his mind. She can't possibly ask this of him. Children would be their resolve. "Please hold fast to your …" she gasped "… to our dream of having children. I will not stop asking God for a miracle."

William's luminous smile returned. "I won't give up if you won't." He pulled her close and smothered her face with kisses. "Work can wait. I've more urgent family matters to tend to. Shall we go upstairs and work on our dream?"

His longing eyes stir in her the passion she once felt when they first met. "Yes. I would love that." Before she knew all else, he had lifted her off the chair and carried her into their bed-chamber. The promise of a brighter and fuller horizon lay ahead.

29

Home Again

T he sound of the team's hooves and the stage coach's wheels broke the midnight silence as it rolled into Snelling. Naomi and William and the other travelers shuffled about collecting themselves and their belongings in the darkened coach as it came to a halt. Eight weeks of train and stagecoach travel would not stop Naomi from returning home. They were met by Ah Teny to bring them to her parent's farm.

"Welcome home, Mr. and Mrs. Tyne. I am your father's houseboy, Ah Teny." He bowed, then grabbed their luggage, and escorted them to the buggy.

The moon's glow reflected off the familiar town structures as they rode past. Jacobi's Mercantile. The Court House. Snelling School. A flood of childhood memories warmed Naomi's heart. However, once the buggy turned onto the wayside path, and the farm came into view, a water pale was not sufficient to contain her tears.

"Darlin', please take my handkerchief and dry your eyes. Your parents will think I've been mistreatin' you." William guffawed, then placed his arm around her shoulder.

Ah Teny pulled the buggy in front of the house, unloaded the couple and their belongings, then directed the horse to the barn.

Huang-Fu greeted and assisted them up the porch. The front door creaked open as her father stood with a kerosene lantern in hand, which cast muted light upon his night-capped smiling face and the foyer entrance.

"Welcome back, Naomi and William," Jonathan said in a hushed voice. "I'm sure you're exhausted from your long journey. Huang-Fu will bring you to your room, and we can catch up in the morning." He kissed Naomi's cheek.

"Thank you, Pa. Good to be home. Yes, we are in need of our nightgowns and sleep."

Jonathan led the way upstairs with the lantern as Huang-Fu retrieved their suitcases. Her old bedroom remained the same as if her parent's enshrined it to her memory. Now it would serve as her and her husband's four-month holiday and family reunion retreat, and for her a reprieve from her humdrum life in Indiana. They fumbled through their luggage, donned their sleeping attire, and climbed in bed. Within minutes William's soft rolling snores, which sounded like the bubbling of hot soup on a stove, bent her ear.

The candle's soft incandescence allowed Naomi to ruminate upon familiar items in her room. Favorite books, Little Folk's Delight, Pictureland, and Alice in Wonderland, perched untouched on a dusty shelf. An old crate that contained her childhood trinkets and games beckoned her to rummage through its contents. She snickered as she recalled the jacks, marbles, wooden spinning tops, sticks, bats, balls, and trundling hoops, which provided hours of entertainment. Too tired to get out of bed, she curled up in the fetal position and pressed her cheek against her embroidered pillowcase fashioned by her own hands many years ago. Multiple memories squeezed through her mind's funnel and soon into her bottled dreams. Tomorrow she shall break that hidden container to release and recapture those moments once more. However, fatigue reigned over her emotion-drenched body, and soon she joined her husband in sweet slumber.

The following morning sunshine danced through the lacy curtains. Now that she had a good night's rest, she threw her covers off and skipped her way to the light. She opened the window and let the country air and bright rays splash all over her. Ah, home again.

The aroma of fresh cut harvest waft into the room as miles of wheat bundles marked the late autumn landscape ready to be thrown onto wagons and hauled over to Nielsen's flour mill. The rhythm of farmworker's voices, the clatter of farm equipment, and the lowing of the mules and horses in preparation for another day's duty harmonized like a well-choreographed symphony. In a few days, Pastor McSwan would come by to bless the harvest before going to market as he's done many times before.

She and William arrived just in time to experience the full harvest on her parent's farm. Baffled by the exhilaration that now ran through her veins, she wondered why the same commotion on William's farm during corn harvest didn't stir in her the same reaction. Joy filled memories of her growing years at Sower Farms, wavered her thoughts as she viewed the property from her second-floor bedroom window. She longed to ride the harvester again with her father and farmhands as the mule-drawn bulky contraption cut, gather, and bundle wheat.

Bouncing back into bed, Naomi cuddled next to her husband and tickled his ears with her warm whispers. "Darlin', shall we rise to meet this most glorious day?" A youthful giggle escaped her. "I'm going to dress and head downstairs for breakfast. Join us when you're ready?"

A sliver of William's pupils peered at her as a slight grimace jerked his lips, then he closed his eyes again. "All right, sweetheart. I'll be down shortly. You go catch up with your family. Just a few more winks."

Naomi searched through her luggage to find a simple cotton frock and apron. She could not wait to linger in the barn to milk the cows and gather eggs for breakfast as she and her sister, Sarah, used to do in their youth. Then after the morning meal, she, Liang, Jia-Li, her mother, and brother, David, would romp around the garden to gather fresh vegetables for lunch and supper. However, Jia-Li and her brother, Samuel, had a home, farm, and garden of their own now. And without doubt, after being gone for two years, her old chores were reassigned to the new houseboy. She hoped to participate once again and enjoy every moment before returning to her queen-like status in Indiana.

Donning her comfy clothes, she ambled downstairs, where familiar voices reverberate from the dining room: Ma, Pa, Liang, Huang-Fu, and David, Clara, and little Isaac. I'm back! She pinched her arm—

home sweet home.

WILLIAM'S MIND NOTED THE WHEAT BUNDLES stack on several wagons as he stood beside his wife and her family under the giant oak tree on the front lawn. The early morning autumn sun cast a clear light upon the faces of Naomi, her parents, Samuel, Sarah, David, their families, and the employees as they gathered to listen to Pastor McSwan bless the harvest. His heart ached as a hint of melancholy transpired upon his wife's disposition. At that moment, her stifled expression seemed as if she arrived at a crossroads to either admire or covet the expanding Sower clan. However, her countenance brightened as the family held hands to pray.

The imaginary dark cloud that once hovered about Naomi in Indiana disappeared and a striking crystal brightness emanate from her as her loved ones surrounded her. He knew he should be pleased for her, yet the obvious precursor to her happiness troubled him. Dear Lord, what are you trying to ask of me? Do you really want me to sell my property and relocate here? Already my wife's constitution is much improved. You'll have to show me far greater signs than this before I endeavor on such an enormous undertaking. He shook his head and closed his eyes, trying to force the thought from his mind and focus on the pastor's message.

"And now Lord, we request Your blessings upon this bounty so that it may sustain us with nourishment and continuous financial provision for an abundant life. We ask this in your Almighty Son, Jesus Christ, the Lord of the harvest. Amen," Pastor McSwan said. The family responded with a hearty amen, and the workers bowed graciously before returning to the fields to gather the remaining bundles and place them in the wagons.

A heavy hand landed on William's shoulder from behind him. He turned and surrendered to his father-in-law's indulgence.

"How would you like to join me for a ride to the flour mill, son?" Jonathan said as plumes of smoke escape between his teeth and pipe accompanied by short spattered coughs. "You can assist me in the price negotiations with Mr. Nielsen."

"Why sure. I'd enjoy that very much." William faced Naomi. "It appears my day has been arranged, dearest. I'll see you when we return." He planted a soft peck upon her brow.

"Of course. How could I refuse such an opportunity for my husband to learn more about the wheat business and better acquaint himself with my father too?" Naomi beamed as her mother came alongside her.

Mary clung to Naomi's elbow. "You fellows take your time. I plan to coerce my daughter for a buggy ride to visit Sower and Son's Farm. If that's all right with her."

Flabbergasted, Naomi near leaped out of her boots. "I was wonderin' when we'd find the time to go. I'm dyin' to see the progress from wheat to almond groves. Samuel tells me its fifty percent complete." She turned to her eldest brother and his expecting wife, Jia-Li. "And congratulations are in order to you both for your second child on the way."

A full grin plastered Samuel's face as he gathered his pregnant wife by his side and shifted his weight to lean on her. "Thank you, sis. I need as much help as I can get to run that place. Might as well be my own." He chuckled.

William noticed a stroke of envy that flutter past Naomi's face. *A child is her greatest desire, Lord. What kind of husband am I not to give her this gift?*

Mary winked and nodded. "Your brother comes from strong Sower stock. He may be scarred with a limp for life, but nothin' will hold him down as long as he has air in his lungs, his wife by his side, and his God guidin' and protectin' them."

William chimed in, "Amen to that!"

Jonathan reached over to Mary and kissed her cheek. "All right, my sweet ladies. We shall see y'all at days end. Enjoy yourselves." He addressed the men about him, "Shall we head over to the wagons?"

30

Strange Dream

The rooster's crow at the slight hint of dawn roused Naomi about the same time every morning for the past two months at Sower Farm. Collecting eggs and milking cows with Ah Teny before the sun peeked over the horizon excited her as it always has during her childhood. She sat up in bed, fumbled for her bedroom slippers in the dark, and changed into her day clothes, all the while trying not to wake her husband. This became her temporary routine once the house boy allowed her to join him in his morning chores that were once hers.

However, this morning a slight queasiness imbalanced her. She took in a deep breath, placed one hand on her abdomen, and the other on the dresser to hold her steady. Last night's dinner wanted to travel up her throat, but she swallowed hard to push its contents back.

Ugh, somethin' didn't agree with me. The chamber pot in the water closet should take care of things. Naomi paused for a moment to collect herself until the nausea subsided, then she continued to dress. With a candle in hand, she exited the bedroom, lit it in the hallway, and meandered to the upstairs bathroom to relieve herself. Returning to normalcy, she headed downstairs to the foyer where Ah Teny was waiting.

"Good morning, Mrs. Tyne. Is everything all right?"

The grandfather clock's hands revealed her arrival time as 5:15 am.

Naomi was late by about fifteen minutes. "I apologize. I had a little trouble, but I'm fine now." She grabbed one of the baskets and milk bucket from his hand. "Shall we go? The animals are waiting for us." A girlish giggle escaped her.

Ah Teny carried a kerosene lantern as she followed him outside toward the barn. A light shade of gray behind the lingering Tule fog lay low on the horizon announcing the arrival of the new day. Oh, how I love this time when no one else is awake except for me, the farm animals, and You, Lord.

They entered the aging wood structure, and each selected a cow to milk. Naomi placed her bucket under the cow's udder and scooted her milking stool to the side where she took a seat. "Hello, girl," she said as she patted the docile beast's side. "Shall we do our mornin' worship? What hymn would you like to hear?"

Naomi leaned in, grabbed hold of the udders, and rested her head on its side. Inhaling deep to begin singing, a strong whiff of the fresh cow patties in the stall touch her nostrils. A sudden rush of nausea and sweat coerced her body. How strange. I'm familiar with these smells. What's wrong with me? I must be ill. Her stomach turned beyond her restrain, and soon she found herself heaving her previous evening's meal on the hay covered floor.

Ah Teny must have heard her for as fast as a cock could fly, he was by her side. "Mrs. Tyne, you are not well. Let me take you back to the house." He held her shaking hands to help her calm and gain control. "Are you able to walk, or shall I carry you?"

After taking a deep breath and wiping her mouth on her sleeve, her strength returned. She leaned into the young man's firm grip and stood slowly to find her balance. "I ... I think my feet can carry me, but I would appreciate your help back to the house. Thank you so much, Teny. Yes, I do believe I need to lie down. I'm sorry I cannot assist you today."

Ah Teny let out controlled laughter, "Oh Mrs. Tyne, no trouble and no need to apologize. Perhaps only upset stomach. Tomorrow you be better. You like me call doctor?"

"Oh, no. That will not be necessary. I'm much improved already. I think a little rest will do me some good."

"All right then. Come. Hold my arm. I will walk you back to

your room." Ah Teny escorted her back to the farmhouse then he returned to the barn.

The room still dark, Naomi used her hands to find her way back to the bed. Once there, she climbed on top of the covers next to her snoring husband. Too weak, she didn't bother to remove her boots or change out of her day clothes. She closed her eyes, fell into a deep sleep, and entered into an unusual and preposterous life.

Bright sunshine cascade into the room along with the bellowing calls of the livestock, which stir Naomi's senses to wake her. She popped up in bed and realized she missed the rooster's crow.

Ah, the cows must be in pain from their swollen udders. Upset at herself, she threw off her covers, climbed into her day clothes, rushed downstairs, grabbed the milk bucket in the kitchen, and then ran to the barn.

Betsy, her favorite cow, stood with round eyes, knees shaking as she belted out long distressed lowing directed at Naomi for her tardiness. If this ol' gal could talk, she'd be casting reprimands at me. After placing the bucket under the creature's udders, the milkmaid sat on her stool and proceeded with the milking process. She rested her head on the cow's bulging side and began singing Midsummer Lullaby.

Silver clouds are lightly sailing
Through the drowsy, trembling air,
And the golden summer sunshine
Casts a glory everywhere.

Naomi tugged on Betsy's udders, and the warm milk trickled from the cow's teats splattering into the bucket. Squirt, squirt. The rhythm moved with the slow melody. Once the container filled with the luscious white liquid, the content animal whipped her tail pleased with her comfort.

Removing the bucket and stool to set them outside of the stall, Naomi then shoveled some feed on a wheelbarrow. Betsy's painful lowing began again accompanied by heavy thumps as if she were stomping the ground.

"I just milked you, Betsy, and I'll have your hay over to you in just a second. Patience girl, patience."

A loud shrill moo from the stall reverberated in the barn, causing

Naomi to move with urgency.

"What can you possibly be complainin' about now?"

Upon her return, she found Betsy lying on the ground licking clean a newborn calf at her side.

"What? Betsy, I didn't know you were pregnant." Upon kneeling, she lifted the calf's head and peered into its dark brown eyes. In her hands, the calf began to morph into a human baby. After the babe gasped for its first breath of air, intense crying proceeded. Startled by the confusing occurrence, the bewildered maiden cradled the infant, rocked it in her arms, and commenced singing the lullaby as she choked on every word.

Softly sob and sigh the billows

As they dream in shadows sweet,

And the swaying reeds and rushes

Kiss the mirror at their feet.

A steady hand shook her shoulders from behind her. "Naomi, darlin', wake up. You're having a bad dream."

The shaking became more aggressive and forced her to open her eyes. The room was sunlit, and William hovered over her. Her heart raced as she pulled her thoughts together. "Oh my darlin', I had the most horrific dream." She sat up in bed and tremble. "Betsy gave birth to a calf. No, a human baby."

"Strange indeed, dear. Betsy's long been dead for some time now. For her to bring a child into the world ... now that's a nightmare."

"What can this mean? Why would I dream of such absurdity?"

William pulled her into his arms. "Now, now, my love. Perhaps being with your growing family is adding pressure to your maternal desires. I think you are over-working yourself. You really don't need to assist Ah Teny with the morning chores."

"Oh no, my husband. Do not suggest that I quit. You know how much I enjoy doing so."

"By the way, why are you still in bed? When I wake, you are usually gone. It seems like you're dressed and ready to go. What happened?"

As the early morning recollections return, so did the nauseating waves. "I went back to bed because I was unwell." Naomi released herself from her husband's hold. Blood left her face, and her belly convulsed even in its empty void. Cold sweat beaded throughout her pale body. "In fact, I'm still not well." She turned to her side and leaned over the bed. Her stomach began to dry heave.

William's strong hand caressed her back. "All right, darlin'. That explains everything. Stay in bed today. I'll have someone go to town and fetch Doctor Cassidy."

GATHERED IN THE PARLOR, William and the family await the physician's prognosis. The staircase creaked as the doctor descended from upstairs. He entered the room, rolled down his sleeves, and adjusted his bifocals. Eager eyes were upon him.

"Naomi must stay in bed for a few days and get plenty of rest," he said with a serious countenance.

William stood and approached the doctor. "What's wrong with her doc?"

"Relax. No need to be alarmed." The doctor guffawed and extended his hand toward the worried husband. "Your wife has an acute case of pregnancy. Let me be the first to congratulate you."

Everyone in the room hushed, jaws gaped.

Shocked by the doctor's prognosis, the father-to-be stammered seeking confirmation. "P, p, pregnant?"

"Yes. Naomi is about six weeks along, and she'll be experiencing morning sickness during her first trimester. Give her plenty of fluids and bland food until she is feeling better."

The room burst into joyful laughter and congratulatory splendor as William's in-laws extended a handshake, slapped his back, and exchanged hugs. It was then that he recalled Naomi's rude awakening that morning. So that's what that dream meant—his inner being radiated, overpowered with felicity.

"Thank you, doctor. May I see her now?"

"Of course, son. Naomi asked me to call all to her room so that you can share in her joy. But make it short, though. She will need her rest."

"Yes, doctor. We will!"

Like cattle stampeding, the entire family rushed to Naomi's bedside.

31

Three Confirmations

The faint scent of ether permeated the waiting room, so Naomi held her handkerchief to her nose to prevent the smell from upsetting her stomach. Dr. Cassidy's clinic had never been a place she desired to visit but had become a necessary appointment while undergoing her first trimester of pregnancy and now entering her second. If not for her weakened state due to the sudden dislike of certain foods and odors, she'd be enjoying this term and progressing without frequent medical observance.

The last month's Christmas merriment at Sower Farms with family traipsed pass her while her days were spent in her bedroom's confines distressed by her fragility. This state deemed unfamiliar to her strong-bodied physique. She struggled like a fish out of water floundering for life. Fighting this unrelenting condition, she forced herself out of bed unless their holiday became a fleeting uneventful moment. With soda crackers in hand and a pot to retch in, she traversed around her parents' home. The fresh air seemed a possible remedy. However, her body's lack of nourishment strained her efforts.

The stabling assistance of her husband's strong arm was her requisite for the regular doctor visitations. Sinewy tan lines in her spouse's face pronounced his strength as she leaned into him while he sat next to her.

They should have gone home two weeks ago but decided to stay another month with the hope of her pregnancy sickness subsiding.

Bert and their employees are more than familiar with the corn sowing regiment and were able to begin without William. However, her husband's eagerness to put his hand to the plow exasperated her every day as he watched the Sower farmhands prepare for their wheat planting season. He did not realize that his pacing on the front porch, while idly staring out into the fields in a state of wanting, added to her stress.

From Naomi's standpoint, her pregnancy occurred during the most appropriate time while on their visit to Snelling, resulting in her husband's undivided attention toward her instead of their farm. The past two years of solitude in Indiana created in her a selfish entitlement. She was so grateful for his support. Misery would have doubled if she were at their home to fend for herself isolated from family and nearby physicians. However, her nagging conscience reprimanded her manner of unfair treatment toward her husband. They had to return home, but how?

Heavens, I never thought child-bearing would be so difficult compared to Sarah's unhindered pregnancies. I guess some women are more natural at being pregnant and giving birth than others. Lord, you certainly did not endow me with that gift! She shook her head in disgrace at the thought.

I'm but skin and bones since this little one inside me took over my body and refuses to eat the food I enjoy. My goodness, when will this nausea subside? Shouldn't I be gaining weight and a small mound appearing on my belly by now? I'm almost five months along.

"Mrs. Tyne, I'll see you now." Dr. Cassidy held the examining door open. His gray slick-back hair certified his years of competent medical experience. A few more wrinkles graced his compassionate brow.

She clung to her husband's elbow. "May William join us?" He hoped to gain the doctor's approval to allow her to return to Indiana. The thought of rugged terrain and the steam locomotive's sway engendered in her troublesome anxiety to further aggravate her condition.

Shrugging his shoulder, the considerate physician volleyed a gentle nod toward them. "Certainly." He motioned as the couple entered. Naomi clung to her husband's arm to assist her. "Please lay down on the examining table, dear."

The doctor proceeded with his routine, checking her vitals, and listening to the baby's heart rate with his stethoscope. "Are you able to hold any food down yet?" he asked.

"A little." She fibbed to suggest her betterment despite the doctor's keen observance.

"Hmm." He extended his hand to Naomi to help her sit upright. "It's not unusual for nausea to extend beyond three months. Some women experience it throughout the entire term of pregnancy."

"Oh, Lord, I hope not. We're supposed to return to Indiana in two weeks," she gasped and held her fingers to her lips. The queasiness began to stir once again. She had always been strong-willed. To be subject to the control of another so small and not yet brought into the world, is a situation she was not accustomed.

"I'm sorry to be the bearer of bad news, Mr. and Mrs. Tyne." His focus latched on William. "Unless your wife regains her appetite and strength, I advise that she not travel and risk the chance of miscarriage. I know the difficulty you both encountered to become pregnant. By the looks of her weakened state now, I doubt that she'll be strong enough in two weeks, let alone the next few months."

At first, William's expression revealed a vacuous countenance as he stood next to his wife and held her hand while solutions seem to race about his head. Then like a strike of lightning, a flash of concern crossed his brow, and his eyes narrow upon Naomi and the future Tyne generation she carried inside her. "Darlin', I will not risk you or our child's life. If you must stay here until the baby is born, then I must oblige. You're in good care with your family and Dr. Cassidy. However, you know as well as I that I must return to oversee the harvest …," he stalled, and a slow and shaky grin crept across his face, "and the sale of the farm."

The room froze for a brief moment as she absorbed her husband's words and allowed it to settle in her head. "What? William, are you sure that is the proper solution? Don't do so on my account. I will be fine, and our little one will keep me well occupied. I promise I shall no longer be melancholy."

William kissed her forehead then searched her soul, his features now radiant and filled with hope. "My darlin' wife, you are my world now, and your family is our only kin. For some time, this thought pressed my mind. I only needed confirmation from God to do so. California's glorious climate and God's will allowed you to become pregnant while in your hometown. That alone is a good sign. To hear the doctor's recommendation for you and our child is, without a doubt, the Lord's determination to open my eyes and relocate us. His response is all around and is as plain as the sun's shine."

Releasing her hand, William walked to the window and peered outside. "After your father shared the scripture God used to call him to move West, I could not get that verse out of my head. It spoke to me like it did your pa."

The doctor followed her husband, his face engaged with an inquisitive expression. "What Bible reference would that be to compel well-established farmers to give up their earthly inheritance and relocate to an unforeseen future?"

"Ah, allow me to quote Genesis 12:1. God spoke to Abraham and said, 'Get out of your country, from your family and from your father's house, to a land that I will show you.'"

"I'm familiar with that passage." The doctor continued reciting verse 2, "'I will make you a great nation; I will bless you and make your name great; and you shall be a blessing.' There is no doubt that God has fulfilled that promise with your father-in-law and will do so for you and Naomi if you heed His call."

William chuckled. "Three confirmations, God's Word, His orchestrated circumstances, and Him speaking through others. What more can I ask for?" He opened the curtain a little wider. "Oh, and one more thing I failed to mention to you, darlin'. There is a magnificent piece of open land between Snelling and La Grange, about 1500 acres, to be exact, that your father brought to my attention. The deed awaits my signature. I can almost see the tall corn growin' in them there fields!"

Within seconds after her husband's announcement, a flutter like the brush of butterfly wings winnowed in her lower abdomen. "Aha!" she cried and let out joyful laughter.

"What is it, my love? Are you all right?" William rushed to her side.

"Oh, yes, sweetheart. I've never felt better while pregnant—our babe dances inside me. I do believe he or she is confirming your decision.

Snelling is where the baby was conceived and will be born." Naomi placed her husband's hand over her belly as the quiver came again. "There. Did you feel that?"

As the sun peeks over the horizon for a new day, so did the glow in William's eyes. "I did, my love. I did!"

"My child, let me introduce you to your pa." For a brief moment, she forgot her weakened condition in the flurry of excitement. Nonetheless, when she stood, her knees buckled, and she fell into her husband's arms. "William, meet your offspring."

A content chuckle escaped him as he embraced her. "I do believe our little one will be as headstrong as his mama. For that, I am well pleased. He needs to be if he is going to take over our farm one day."

Dr. Cassidy held the door open as William scooped his wife into his arms and carried her to the carriage. "Continue to get plenty of rest and nourishment, Naomi. Until your next visit."

"Thank you, doctor!"

32

Jolly Good Fellow

Strolling in the orchard's shade at Sower and Sons Farm, Jonathan and Samuel inspected the abundant fuzzy fruit. Early summer and the almond tree limbs weighed heavy with clusters of pale green pods transformed from spring's pretty white blossoms with magenta centers. The once dense floral aroma that attracted an abundance of bees dissipated, giving way to the sun's high heat. In due time the pod's hulls will become leathery and cracked, exposing its exotic crunchy treat to be harvested in autumn.

Jonathan pulled a pod off one of the clusters and used his pocket knife to cut into the hull, revealing the hard shell inside, which protected the immature almond within. He shook his head in amazement and quote Genesis 1:11, "And God said, 'Let the earth bring forth grass, the herb yielding seed, *and* the fruit tree yielding fruit after his kind, whose seed *is* in itself, upon the earth: and it was so.'" A wide grin cast upon his face. Jonathan passed the immature nut into Samuel's hand as his son hobbled alongside him.

"Pa, I do believe we will see a great almond harvest this year now that the trees are mature." Samuel tossed the open pod above him as if it were a firecracker exploding on a grand occasion.

"It sure is looking that way. We shall reap the fruit of our labors from this orchard for the first time. The Almighty God is a good Father. Our family's blessings continue to abound."

Hearty laughter expelled from Samuel's lungs. "In more ways than one, I suppose. Every branch of our family tree is producing a harvest too." He winked.

The clay pipe in Jonathan's shirt pocket beckoned him like the sweet aroma of incense. He retrieved it and a small tobacco tin from his trousers, opened it, grabbed a pinch, and stuffed it in the pipe's bowl. Upon lighting it, he inhaled a few deep breaths to partake of its alluring and pungent balm. He wheezed as smoke passed his lips when he spoke.

"Yep. Soon you and Jia-Li will be neck-and-neck with Sarah and Lad and have a small cluster of children of your own. Now that Evelyn is born, you only need one more offspring."

"Well, Pa, I'll leave that decision in God's hands. For now, we'll spend our attention on the two precious blossoms He's already given us." Samuel paused and turned to his father. "By the way, isn't Naomi due to deliver any day now?"

"Yes, and I … we … in fact, our entire household can't wait till she does. I believe your poor sister is the most miserable pregnant woman on God's green earth. Although her appetite has returned, her sickness continues to trouble her."

Jonathan stopped and placed his hands on his hips, grimacing. "We've been aiding her hand and foot. Dr. Cassidy makes home visits since her belly is as big as a barn, and she can barely stand on her own two feet."

As he moved forward, the aging father wagged his boney finger. "Thank the Lord, Naomi inherited the strong genes from my side of the family. If it were Sarah with this problem, she would've only given birth to one. Let's pray Naomi will want more children after this ordeal is over."

Samuel wiped the moisture on his forehead with his cotton coat's sleeve. He popped the cork off the water bottle, which hung in a woven basket on his belt, took a sip, and then handed it to Jonathan to do the same. "I'm so glad William made it back to California in time to witness the birth of his firstborn. That is a moment any first father should not pass over."

The cringe on Samuel's face betrayed his efforts to conceal the pain in his crippled leg as he turned. "Had I not been mending, I might've missed my son's first breath into this world. Knowing my inability to stay in one place for too long, I probably would've been tending to some other matter when Jia-Li went into labor." He snickered. "God does use all things for good for those who love Him ... even my unfortunate circumstance. Perhaps my tragedy is what it took to slow me down a bit to appreciate God's blessings. Especially the birth of my children and my precious wife's crowning and most arduous moment."

After taking a swig of the tepid drink, the weathered father returned the bottle to his seasoned son. "Well, the good news is you survived to take part in your beautiful family's lives."

Jonathan continued to stroll beneath the cool of the trees. "Thank the Lord for watching over William too. God knew all along who the corn farm's new owner would be. Someone who appreciated his kin folk's farm, understood the corn business well, and gave him the level of comfort needed to pass his inheritance on to someone he could trust with his ancestor's legacy."

"Oh, and who might that be?"

"His head supervisor, Bert, purchased your brother-in-law's farm. Apparently, he had been saving his earnings for some time with the hope of purchasing his own acreage one day. To his amazement, he never thought it would be the property that he grew up in and worked with his parents."

"Well, that is a blessing, indeed."

"You bet." Jonathan removed his tattered sweat-stained slouch hat to wipe his brow. "William received other offers higher than Bert's. The rows of emerging corn stalks are quite impressive for a turn-key farming operation. However, in his heart, Bert bid the most deserving of all the candidates. In the end, your brother-in-law did well for himself."

"That is fantastic news, indeed. Now all he must do is purchase the acreage on La Grange Road and build his farmhouse. Then they are set." Samuel slapped his knee.

The thought of purchasing land caused Jonathan to stop and view the estate at the end of the orchard, which he owned. It served as Samuel and his family's home, which would be their future inheritance. Fully operational upon his purchase, this farm had fewer difficulties establishing than the fields he had to settle at Sower Farms. "Easier said than done. That acreage is virgin territory. You may recall what we had to do to break up our fallow ground when we first arrived in Snelling."

"Sakes alive. I do remember." Samuel huffed at the thought. "We all near broke our backs for that property." Chuckling at his pun, he shook his cane. "You put us all to work. Even David, as young as he was, worked the land."

Jonathan bent on his knee, gather a handful of dirt in his fist, crushed it in his palm, and let it fall back to the earth. The fertile San Joaquin soil fared well to produce crops, after removing the weeds and rocks. Memories of difficult circumstances he, his young family, and his farmworkers endured to clear and prepare the land for agriculture almost fifteen years earlier caused his heart to race.

"I paved the way for my children as shall William for his family's namesake."

In the distance, the faint sound of the Merced River pushing through to the San Joaquin Valley floor comforted him. "Water shortage never was an issue for my farms and shouldn't be for William and Naomi's property either with Lake Don Pedro nearby. They must do the same and dig for well water to irrigate their crops. It may be a couple of years before they'll see any profit.

"Good thing he is still young, and his back is strong." Jonathan peered up at the striking contrast of Samuel leaning on his cane.

Were all the hardships my family endured to come to California worth it? Jonathan's eyes scan the vast property sustaining not only his kin but the states growing population as well. Yes indeed. Lord, you never said it would be an easy task. You fulfilled Your promise to me. You brought me to a new land, increased my household, and blessed others through our obedience to You.

Contentment filled Jonathan's heart. As he stood, an unusual heaviness pressed on his lungs. He lurched. His pipe fell from his mouth, and he wrapped his arms around his rib cage.

As his father toppled to the ground, Samuel dropped his cane and stumbled to his side to hold him. "Pa, are you all right?"

Gasping for air, Jonathan clung to Samuel's arm as he searched his thoughts to explain the horrendous agony he felt in his chest without alarming his son. "Give me a moment, Sam. I'll be all right. I, I think it's my ol' war wound." He let out a pain-filled chortle. "The recollections of our early days must've triggered it."

Samuel removed his sack coat, rolled it, and placed it under his father's head. "I thought that thorn in your side healed a long time ago. Well, Pa, be still and relax now. Don't worry about a thing."

Jonathan could not utter a word as his son loosened his collar, unbuttoned his shirt, and placed his head on his chest to hear his heartbeat.

"Pa, you're going to need to muster up some of your family strength and lie here for a moment while I go get help. Now I want you to think about your grandchildren and all the birthday celebrations ahead. Let's leave the past behind us. We have the future to look forward to now. And what a glorious one it shall be." Samuel's warm smile concealed the worry in his eyes. "All right, find that strength, Pa. I'll be back in a few minutes. Will you do that for me?"

Jonathan nodded and closed his eyes as he listened to his eldest scramble away at a rapid shuffling pace. He forced himself to envision the faces of his grandbabies. Amanda, Billy, Isabel, Adam, Evelyn, Isaac, and baby Tyne, who was not yet born. Seven precious children whom he needed to spend time with and adore.

Oh, dear Lord. Will you give me the years to grow old and gray with my family? Moisture formed under his eyelids as a well-lit homemade birthday cake came into his mind's view. He tried counting the tiny lights, but there were too many ablaze. Wait a minute. Amanda is only nine. There are well over fifty candles on that cake.

His entire household surrounded him and began singing.

For he's a jolly good fellow,
For he's a jolly good fellow,
For he's a jolly good fellow,
For nobody can deny.

His wife hugged his neck. Make a wish, Jonny!

As he blew on the flames, his vision darkened, and fatigue overtook him.

33

Goodly Heritage

Lying in bed next to her comatose husband, Mary kissed his cheek then pulled the bed covers tightly around them both. The warm night air drifted in their opened window carrying with it the scent of roses from the flower bed below. The shimmer from the full moon and stars filled their room like a sprinkling of angel's dust in a hemisphere of darkness.

In all their years, she had never stopped to measure the lines on Jonathan's sun-weathered face. She touched the deep crevices which spread from his eye's corners. The night shadows intensified wrinkles on his brow, and without surprise to her, on her aged hands as well.

Whispered conversation flowed from her lips to his ear. "My love, the years flew by without warnin' us. Like a night thief, it stole our youth." She combed through the grays on his head and beard. "Our children are grown with families of their own now. Our job is done to raise them the best we could with the provisions God gave us. He has blessed us with much for His glory. For that, I'm forever grateful.

"My darlin' husband, you've accomplished much on our spiritual journey with the Lord to California. You can rest knowin' you have taken good care of your family. Without a doubt, your father and grandfather are mighty proud of you in completin' the Sower legacy they begun."

She turned on her back and held Jonathan's hand at his side as she prayed.

"Dear Lord, the past three days, my body and soul withers beside my husband to whom I am made one flesh through Your divine appointment. I plead to You, and still, he does not wake. Dr. Cassidy has done all he knows to do. Jonathan is now in your capable hands. Father, if it is your will, please bring him back to me. I don't know if I could live without him. I love him so. His family adores him, and he is yet to see all his grandchildren come into this world. My lips shall fast and pray as I await Your decision, Lord. Amen."

Mary opened her eyes and lay her head on Jonathan's chest with the least amount of pressure. Beats from his heart were slow and faint, along with the slight rise and fall of his lungs.

"Please wake, my darlin'. I'm here waitin' for you and will never leave your side." She wiped the tears from her sore eyes.

The intense bereavement consumed her body's need for nourishment and unbeknownst to her, her health began to falter as the fourth day of fasting advent. The door locked, she ignored her family's plea to allow them entrance and provide sustenance. Her wedding vows played in her head like the continuous cricket song that lulled her weakening body, soul, and spirit to sleep.

I, Mary Grace Baker, take you, Jonathan Stephen Sower, for my lawful husband, to have and to hold from this day forward, for better, for worse, for richer, for poorer, in sickness and health, until death do us part.

ALMOST A WEEK LATER, the late afternoon sun hung low over Snelling Cemetery as family and friends gathered around the coffins of the beloved patriarch and successful land baron, Jonathan Sower, and his loving and faithful wife, Mary. David discovered their deceased bodies at rest in their beds on the fourth morning after his father's fatal heart attack. Their amorous and peaceful facial expressions foretold their life's commitment to one another. In his mind's eye, David pictured his father waiting at Heaven's gate for his beloved wife to arrive so that they may enter hand-in-hand as they have done together on earth through all their endeavors.

As multitudes arrived from nearby county towns, the aspiring preacher, still numb from the sudden death of his parents, placed his trembling hand over his heart overwhelmed by the community's outpouring of love and condolences. He adjusted his cravat as he sat in a front row with his siblings arranged for the immediate family under a canvas fly. The open graves and amber-colored wooden coffins engraved with the Lord's cross on the covers seem to float on a bed of flowers graced by those who mourned their parents' passing.

Samuel sat on David's right, posture erect, steel-faced, holding his composure using all the family strength he can muster. Beside him, Sarah whimpered. To his left, with vigor Naomi fan herself doing her best to control her emotions and discomfort as she wept. With a heavy heart, David thumbed through his notes in his Bible. An empty silence fell upon their spouses and children seated behind them.

Tangled nerves distraught David as he reached for his watch in his coat pocket. "Three o'clock. Time to address the crowd." Glancing at his somber family, his legs walked toward the simple wooden podium beside the caskets as his mind and soul followed as if delayed. He did his best to arrest the bubbling surge boiling from deep within like molten preserves in a pressurized canister.

Temperance. His sermon notes prod him. Control your emotions. You must deliver this vital funeral message for two of the most prodigious people in your life.

His mouth opened as he allowed the Holy Spirit to speak through him and give him strength. "'Honor thy father and thy mother: that thy days may be long upon the land which the LORD thy God giveth thee.' This commandment was the fifth of ten that God gave to His people. It followed the first four commands which pertained to Himself and how we should revere and respect Him. Of the ten, eight of His instructions addressed things we 'shall not' do, and two regarded honoring Him our Heavenly Father and the next closest image of Him, our earthly parents.

"The concept of Godly parenting defines His relationship with us His children. He is the ultimate Father, for He created us. His desire for His children is best explained in Jeremiah 29:11, where God tells us, 'For I know the thoughts that I think toward you, saith the LORD, thoughts of peace, and not of evil, to give you an expected end.'

"What would children hope to expect from their parents? Unconditional love, joy, peace, longsuffering, gentleness, goodness, faith, meekness, temperance. Galatians 5:22 tells us that these are the Holy Spirits' characteristics, which He passes on to us to practice. These are foundational mannerisms that we can maintain to live life peaceably with others.

"Take heed, for He has never promised us wealth, fame, or glory. However, if we obey His commandments and do what is right, then the circumstantial outcome is longer, peaceful lives. Isn't that what we should strive for? Shouldn't this be what is important to us and not the temporal things of this world, which we cannot bring with us into eternity?

"This is something my parents hoped to attain through their love and submission to the Lord. They wanted to do right by Him and for their family. Through their righteous obedience, all goodly consequence followed through His divine laws.

"My father and mother, like all of us, struggled with human frailties. Unlike God, who is omnipotent, omnipresent, and omniscient, my parents did their best as humanly possible. They had four children, a large farm, and numerous employees under their care. They could not be everywhere at the same time or obtain the foreknowledge of things to come, nor develop the supernatural strength to accomplish all that needed to be done. However, they had faith in a God and Father who could.

"And so they put their trust in Him and also taught their children to do so as well. That is the most endearing gift and lesson a child can receive from their believing parents. In Matthew 24:35, Jesus tells us, 'Heaven and earth shall pass away, but my words shall not pass away.' His promises will live forever. We can trust Him in that.

"Of His covenants the greatest was this to us when Jesus said in regards to Himself in John 3:16, 'For God so loved the world that He gave his only begotten Son, that whosoever believeth in Him should not perish, but have everlasting life.' This precious faith is what my parents believed in wholeheartedly and were diligent and obedient to pass it on to their children."

David scanned the horizon at the bountiful legacy his parents built and left behind for their family. His focus then rested on his heartbroken siblings, their spouses and children, and the community of friends that surrounded them.

"The fruit of the Lord's righteousness is seen all around us not only in the temporal necessities, but in the love we have for one another for our immediate family and for our neighbors too. Jesus summed up all the commandments into two in Matthew 22:37-39, *'You shall love the LORD your God with all your heart, with all your soul, and with all your mind.* This is *the* first and great commandment. And *the* second *is* like it: *You shall love your neighbor as yourself.'*

"And this is why all of you gather at my beloved parents' gravesite today to give them the honor and respect due them. For you are recipients of the love and affection from this fine godly couple to whose end there are no bounds because of their everlasting relationship with our Lord and King, Jesus. Their absence will impact us all. May they both rest in eternal peace in the arms of our Father in Heaven. And now I shall read Psalm 16, my parents' final request in their Will and Testament." David opened his Bible and read aloud.

"Preserve me, O God: for in Thee do I put my trust.

O my soul, thou hast said unto the LORD, Thou *art* my Lord: my goodness *extendeth* not to Thee; b*ut* to the saints that *are* in the earth, and *to* the excellent, in whom *is* all my delight.

Their sorrows shall be multiplied *that* hasten *after* another *god*: their drink offerings of blood will I not offer, nor take up their names into my lips.

The LORD *is* the portion of mine inheritance and of my cup: Thou maintainest my lot.

The lines are fallen unto me in pleasant *places*; yea, I have a goodly heritage.

I will bless the LORD, who hath given me counsel: my reins also instruct me in the night seasons.

I have set the LORD always before me: because *He is* at my right hand, I shall not be moved.

Therefore my heart is glad, and my glory rejoiceth: my flesh also shall rest in hope.

For Thou wilt not leave my soul in hell; neither wilt Thou suffer thine Holy One to see corruption.

Thou wilt shew me the path of life: in thy presence *is* fulness of joy; at thy right hand *there are* pleasures for evermore."

34

Introductions

"Your grandpa Jonathan crafted this tin star many years ago for our family's first Christmas tree when we arrived in California in 1864." Naomi removed ornaments from the crate containing decorations her mother collected through the years and dangled them before her nephew, Isaac. She handed the keepsake to David, who climbed a chair, placed the orb atop the fresh pine, and lit the candle behind the celestial piece as he had done as a child. Streaks of dazzling light jut through the many precise nail-pierced holes about its cavity. He marveled at his three-year-old son's eyes glistening at the brilliant display.

"Shall we hang the cookies we baked, son?" Clara said, holding a tray full of sugary delights. "Come, darling husband. Help us, will you? The tree must be ready before the rest of the family arrive this evening for Christmas Eve dinner."

Naomi sat beside William by the hearth and leaned her head upon his shoulder. "Seems like eons since all of us lived in Indiana. Now here we are about to begin our new lives in Snelling with our own families just as Pa and Ma did fifteen years ago."

Patting his wife's hand and kissing her head, William cast his sights on David's sweet young family as they trim the tree. "Imagine, darlin', next year this time we'll be in our new farmhouse decorating our home with our children. If your parents were alive, they'd be amazed at how far we've progressed since our decision to relocate to Snelling earlier this year."

"Yes. How did you ever read my thoughts?" The imagery of their new property on La Grange Road appeared in her mind.

A sarcastic chortle escaped her husband. "I'm your husband, and we are one flesh. Are we not?" His question was more of a statement.

"My portion of my inheritance will carry us for a year or two until our crops establish themselves. The steady funds will allow us to take our time to build and set our plans right," Naomi said.

David paused and turned to address her. "There is no rush for you to leave. After all, Pa and Ma left Sower Farms to be divided equally between me, you, and Sarah, plus an extra portion to whomever of us chooses to reside here and manage the business."

Erect on the sofa, Naomi shrugged her shoulder and responded with a warm smile. "Had I been a lonely spinster, I would've been the obvious candidate for the task to maintain the good family name. May I remind you, I'm a Tyne now, Sarah a Hampton, and Samuel inherited S&S Farm, now renamed Samuel Sower Farm. So by process of elimination, you, David Sower, must continue the legacy."

David inhaled deep and stumbled to find his father's old wingback chair to sit down. "I, I never expected this. Please don't misunderstand me, for I am grateful indeed. The inheritance is security for my family. However, I cannot handle this business in moderation. What will become of my plans to minister? How will I do both?"

Finger wagging, Naomi knelt beside her bewildered brother. "Where there is a will, there is a way. You will not be alone to oversee Sower Farm's progress. As partners, Sarah and I shall assist you. Our best interest is at stake. Besides, the business, for all intent and purposes, operates by itself. The loyal staff of employees are experts in the wheat industry."

Philippians 4:6-7 crossed her mind sent by the Holy Spirit. "Be careful for nothing; but in everything by prayer and supplication with thanksgiving let your requests be made known unto God. And the peace of God, which passeth all understanding, shall keep your hearts and minds through Christ Jesus."

Nodding at her words of comfort, David turned his focus on Clara and Isaac and resumed trimming the tree. "Ah, somehow, I sense God will be testing me. Dividing my time between ministry, my family, and Sower Farms will be a challenge. All right, then I'm up to the task as long as you and Sarah are by my side." He winked at his sister.

"You can count on me as Pa has in the past," Naomi said when a faint cry came from a bassinet. "Speaking of which, I made plans today for my family to visit Pa and Ma's gravesite to introduce them to the latest addition to our Sower clan. I've meant to do so for some time now. However, as you know, little time was afforded me to break away. This afternoon shall be the appointed moment before this evening's dinner. Would you mind, David and Clara?"

Naomi's sister-in-law wrapped a couple of cookies in a napkin and handed them to her. "Not at all. As the new occupants of Sower Farms, I suppose I'll have to get used to managing the household and supporting my husband's endeavors. I've much to learn from your mother." She giggled. "If only my mother and father were here to see me now. Their little Clara is living on a grand farm such as this. Say a little prayer for us, too, as you visit your parents."

"Thank you. Yes, we will. Until we return then."

NAOMI'S HEART RACED as the carriage turned right headed west on Merced Falls Road from Sower Farms' wayside path. The last time she traversed this path was six months earlier while grief-stricken over her parents' death and so close to the end of her last trimester of pregnancy. The guilt of not visiting their gravesite as her other siblings and their families chose to do press on her mind. Circumstances dictate her availability, and now that all events have calmed, she made sure to visit them. What better time than Christmas Eve? *My little surprise will be my gift to Pa and Ma.*

As William drove, Naomi craned her neck to capture the town from a distance. First, they passed by Snelling School, where imagery of her and her dearest young friends flit about playing games in the yard like happy ghosts from her past. At the town's edge, she shielded her eyes from the low hanging winter sun to view the silhouette of Snelling Courthouse and Jacobi's Mercantile still standing proudly in the center of town.

A shiver ran down her back as she recalled the winks and snickers between Mr. Jacobi, Marshal Warner, Deputy Jamison, and Margaret the county clerk upon her arrest when she was caught stealing from the mercantile. Wink. Wink? Realization and understanding finally donned on her. They suspected all along that youngsters were behind this mischief. Imprisoning minors did not possess their hearts because they had bigger fish to fry than dealing with misguided school children. In particular, one young lady who comes from a well-bred Christian family. She shook her head in dismay. With the best of their ability, they taught me a grand lesson by scarin' the livin' daylight out of me! A loud chuckle escaped her.

"What's so funny?" William asked as he pulled into Snelling Cemetery.

"Oh, don't mind me, darlin'. I was reminiscing over silly childhood moments. One day I'll be sure to tell you all about that time."

"All right. Well, we're here." He parked the carriage close to her parents' plots. "Why don't you go ahead and we'll catch up. I know you want to have a private moment with them. When you're ready, wave to me, and we shall join you."

"Thank you, William. You are a dear indeed for understanding. I shouldn't be long." Naomi touched his cheek and kissed his lips.

"Allow me to help you down." Her husband stepped off the carriage and assisted her. He reached behind the front bench seat, grabbed two floral bouquets, and placed them in her arms. "All right, I'll be waiting for your signal."

She nodded, turned, and walked toward the gravesites.

The oak trees were almost bare. Much of the foliage had fallen covering the ground in a blanket of brown wither. A swirl of wind brushed Naomi's face, touched her bonnet's feather, and moved her bustled skirt's hem. Dry leaves scattered past her as she approached the plots now covered with manicured grass and each adorned with gracious yet humble headstones with her parents' names, the date of their birth and death, and a brief description which sum up their amazing life story.

Naomi placed the bouquets by their headstones and found space on the lawn between the two plots to seat herself.

"Hello, Pa and Ma. I hope you'll forgive me for not visiting sooner." She looked down at her hands and twiddled her thumbs. Even though her parents were in heaven, their presence seemed to be staring at her from their headstones. Her guilt kept her from looking up.

"After giving birth, I had to nurse. Then after a few months, William and I were inundated with purchasing our property and making arrangements to build our farmhouse." She lifted her chin as she shared her good news. "Yes, we did it. We plan to call our place Boulder Farms because of all the boulders we will have to clear before we can plant anything there." She laughed. "The hard work will be worth our effort, though. The property is beautiful, and the ground rich and fertile. You would have approved, Pa."

She shifted her legs beneath her and continued. "Afterwards, the harvest began, and without you leading the way Pa, David, Sarah, and I fumbled through the process. Thank God, you trained your employees well. They initiated their seasoned practice. William and Samuel took the reins when bringing the wheat to Nielsen's Flour Mill and dealt with negotiations. All went well, and business is operating as smooth as normal. You would be very proud of us."

Naomi tugged at the blade of grass at her feet. "Before I could catch my breath, the holidays were upon us." Thoughts of Christmas past played her heartstrings. "I miss you both so much." Tears welled up, and her throat ran dry. "I wished you were here when I gave birth and now to enjoy the festivities with my family. Now you'll have to wait some time before you meet my children in person," she paused, "in heaven one day." She stood, brushed the grass off her skirt, and waved at her husband, who waited by the carriage.

"Yes, Ma, you heard me right. You shall always be the school teacher at heart. I recall our endless days of grammar and mathematics at home under your loving tutorage. I did use the plural 'children' in the correct manner."

Two large baskets in his hands, William arrived with a jovial expression. He placed them on the ground, and both he and Naomi scooped up two babies wrapped in swaddling clothes. "Pa, Ma, I want you to meet the newest members of your family. Yes, I had twins. No wonder I was sick all the time and as big as a barn." She laughed and pulled the blanket away from the baby's faces.

"This little boy is named after both his grandfathers. His name is Franklin Jonathan Tyne. And this little girl carries her grandmother's names, Mary Ellen Tyne. Merry Christmas."

The Parable of the Enemy Sowing Tares

Matthew 13:24-30

²⁴ Another parable put he forth unto them, saying, The kingdom of heaven is likened unto a man which sowed good seed in his field:

²⁵ But while men slept, his enemy came and sowed tares among the wheat, and went his way.

²⁶ But when the blade was sprung up, and brought forth fruit, then appeared the tares also.

²⁷ So the servants of the householder came and said unto him, Sir, didst not thou sow good seed in thy field? from whence then hath it tares?

²⁸ He said unto them, An enemy hath done this. The servants said unto him, Wilt thou then that we go and gather them up?

²⁹ But he said, Nay; lest while ye gather up the tares, ye root up also the wheat with them.

³⁰ Let both grow together until the harvest: and in the time of harvest I will say to the reapers, Gather ye together first the tares, and bind them in bundles to burn them: but gather the wheat into my barn.

What Comes Out of the Mouth Defiles the Man

Matthew 15:10-20

¹⁰ And he called the multitude, and said unto them, Hear, and understand:

¹¹ Not that which goeth into the mouth defileth a man; but that which cometh out of the mouth, this defileth a man.

¹² Then came his disciples, and said unto him, Knowest thou that the Pharisees were offended, after they heard this saying?

¹³ But he answered and said, Every plant, which my heavenly Father hath not planted, shall be rooted up.

¹⁴ Let them alone: they be blind leaders of the blind. And if the blind lead the blind, both shall fall into the ditch.

¹⁵ Then answered Peter and said unto him, Declare unto us this parable.

¹⁶ And Jesus said, Are ye also yet without understanding?

¹⁷ Do not ye yet understand, that whatsoever entereth in at the mouth goeth into the belly, and is cast out into the draught?

¹⁸ But those things which proceed out of the mouth come forth from the heart; and they defile the man.

¹⁹ For out of the heart proceed evil thoughts, murders, adulteries, fornications, thefts, false witness, blasphemies:

²⁰ These are the things which defile a man: but to eat with unwashen hands defileth not a man.

The Parable of the Leased Vineyard

Matthew 21:33-41

³³ Hear another parable: There was a certain householder, which planted a vineyard, and hedged it round about, and digged a winepress in it, and built a tower, and let it out to husbandmen, and went into a far country:

³⁴ And when the time of the fruit drew near, he sent his servants to the husbandmen, that they might receive the fruits of it.

³⁵ And the husbandmen took his servants, and beat one, and killed another, and stoned another.

³⁶ Again, he sent other servants more than the first: and they did unto them likewise.

³⁷ But last of all he sent unto them his son, saying, They will reverence my son.

³⁸ But when the husbandmen saw the son, they said among themselves, This is the heir; come, let us kill him, and let us seize on his inheritance.

³⁹ And they caught him, and cast him out of the vineyard, and slew him.

⁴⁰ When the lord therefore of the vineyard cometh, what will he do unto those husbandmen?

⁴¹ They say unto him, He will miserably destroy those wicked men, and

will let out his vineyard unto other husbandmen, which shall render him the fruits in their seasons.

The Parable of the Fig Tree

Matthew 24:32-35

³² Now learn a parable of the fig tree; When his branch is yet tender, and putteth forth leaves, ye know that summer is nigh:

³³ So likewise ye, when ye shall see all these things, know that it is near, even at the doors.

³⁴ Verily I say unto you, This generation shall not pass, till all these things be fulfilled.

³⁵ Heaven and earth shall pass away, but my words shall not pass away.

The Parable of New and Old Garments and Wineskins

Luke 5:33-39

³³ And they said unto him, Why do the disciples of John fast often, and make prayers, and likewise the disciples of the Pharisees; but thine eat and drink?

³⁴ And he said unto them, Can ye make the children of the bridechamber fast, while the bridegroom is with them?

³⁵ But the days will come, when the bridegroom shall be taken away from them, and then shall they fast in those days.

³⁶ And he spake also a parable unto them; No man putteth a piece of a new garment upon an old; if otherwise, then both the new maketh a rent, and the piece that was taken out of the new agreeth

not with the old.

³⁷ And no man putteth new wine into old bottles; else the new wine will burst the bottles, and be spilled, and the bottles shall perish.

³⁸ But new wine must be put into new bottles; and both are preserved.

³⁹ No man also having drunk old wine straightway desireth new: for he saith, The old is better.

The Parable of the Man who was Rich with Treasures and not of God

Luke 12:13-34

¹³ And one of the company said unto him, Master, speak to my brother, that he divide the inheritance with me.

¹⁴ And he said unto him, Man, who made me a judge or a divider over you?

¹⁵ And he said unto them, Take heed, and beware of covetousness: for a man's life consisteth not in the abundance of the things which he possesseth.

¹⁶ And he spake a parable unto them, saying, The ground of a certain rich man brought forth plentifully:

¹⁷ And he thought within himself, saying, What shall I do, because I have no room where to bestow my fruits?

¹⁸ And he said, This will I do: I will pull down my barns, and build greater; and there will I bestow all my fruits and my goods.

¹⁹ And I will say to my soul, Soul, thou hast much goods laid up for many years; take thine ease, eat, drink, and be merry.

²⁰ But God said unto him, Thou fool, this night thy soul shall be required of thee: then whose shall those things be, which thou hast provided?

²¹ So is he that layeth up treasure for himself, and is not rich toward God.

²² And he said unto his disciples, Therefore I say unto you, Take no thought for your life, what ye shall eat; neither for the body, what ye shall put on.

²³ The life is more than meat, and the body is more than raiment.

²⁴ Consider the ravens: for they neither sow nor reap; which neither have storehouse nor barn; and God feedeth them: how much more are ye better than the fowls?

²⁵ And which of you with taking thought can add to his stature one cubit?

²⁶ If ye then be not able to do that thing which is least, why take ye thought for the rest?

²⁷ Consider the lilies how they grow: they toil not, they spin not; and yet I say unto you, that Solomon in all his glory was not arrayed like one of these.

²⁸ If then God so clothe the grass, which is to day in the field, and to morrow is cast into the oven; how much more will he clothe you, O ye of little faith?

²⁹ And seek not ye what ye shall eat, or what ye shall drink, neither be ye of doubtful mind.

³⁰ For all these things do the nations of the world seek after: and your Father knoweth that ye have need of these things.

³¹ But rather seek ye the kingdom of God; and all these things shall be added unto you.

³² Fear not, little flock; for it is your Father's good pleasure to give you the kingdom.

³³ Sell that ye have, and give alms; provide yourselves bags which wax not old, a treasure in the heavens that faileth not, where no thief approacheth, neither moth corrupteth.

³⁴ For where your treasure is, there will your heart be also.

The Parable of Whoever Exalts Himself Will Be Humbled

Luke 14:7-14

⁷ And he put forth a parable to those which were bidden, when he marked how they chose out the chief rooms; saying unto them.

⁸ When thou art bidden of any man to a wedding, sit not down in the highest room; lest a more honourable man than thou be bidden of him;

⁹ And he that bade thee and him come and say to thee, Give this man place; and thou begin with shame to take the lowest room.

¹⁰ But when thou art bidden, go and sit down in the lowest room; that when he that bade thee cometh, he may say unto thee, Friend, go up higher: then shalt thou have worship in the presence of them that sit at meat with thee.

¹¹ For whosoever exalteth himself shall be abased; and he that humbleth himself shall be exalted.

¹² Then said he also to him that bade him, When thou makest a dinner or a supper, call not thy friends, nor thy brethren, neither thy kinsmen, nor thy rich neighbours; lest they also bid thee again, and a recompence be made thee.

¹³ But when thou makest a feast, call the poor, the maimed, the lame, the blind:

¹⁴ And thou shalt be blessed; for they cannot recompense thee: for thou shalt be recompensed at the resurrection of the just.

The Pharisee and the Tax Collector

Luke 18:9-14

⁹ And he spake this parable unto certain which trusted in themselves that they were righteous, and despised others:

¹⁰ Two men went up into the temple to pray; the one a Pharisee, and the other a publican.

¹¹ The Pharisee stood and prayed thus with himself, God, I thank thee, that I am not as other men are, extortioners, unjust, adulterers, or even as this publican.

¹² I fast twice in the week, I give tithes of all that I possess.

¹³ And the publican, standing afar off, would not lift up so much as his eyes unto heaven, but smote upon his breast, saying, God be

merciful to me a sinner.

¹⁴ I tell you, this man went down to his house justified rather than the other: for every one that exalteth himself shall be abased; and he that humbleth himself shall be exalted.

The Parable of Finishing What You Built

Luke 14:25-35

²⁵ And there went great multitudes with him: and he turned, and said unto them,

²⁶ If any man come to me, and hate not his father, and mother, and wife, and children, and brethren, and sisters, yea, and his own life also, he cannot be my disciple.

²⁷ And whosoever doth not bear his cross, and come after me, cannot be my disciple.

²⁸ For which of you, intending to build a tower, sitteth not down first, and counteth the cost, whether he have sufficient to finish it?

²⁹ Lest haply, after he hath laid the foundation, and is not able to finish it, all that behold it begin to mock him,

³⁰ Saying, This man began to build, and was not able to finish.

³¹ Or what king, going to make war against another king, sitteth not down first, and consulteth whether he be able with ten thousand to meet him that cometh against him with twenty thousand?

³² Or else, while the other is yet a great way off, he sendeth an ambassage, and desireth conditions of peace.

³³ So likewise, whosoever he be of you that forsaketh not all that he hath, he cannot be my disciple.

³⁴ Salt is good: but if the salt have lost his savour, wherewith shall it be seasoned?

³⁵ It is neither fit for the land, nor yet for the dunghill; but men cast it out. He that hath ears to hear, let him hear.

The Parable of Faithful Praying

Luke 18:1-7

1 And he spake a parable unto them to this end, that men ought always to pray, and not to faint;
2 Saying, There was in a city a judge, which feared not God, neither regarded man:
3 And there was a widow in that city; and she came unto him, saying, Avenge me of mine adversary.
4 And he would not for a while: but afterward he said within himself, Though I fear not God, nor regard man;
5 Yet because this widow troubleth me, I will avenge her, lest by her continual coming she weary me.
6 And the Lord said, Hear what the unjust judge saith.
7 And shall not God avenge his own elect, which cry day and night unto him, though he bear long with them?

Goodly Heritage

Psalm 16

1 Preserve me, O God: for in thee do I put my trust.
2 O my soul, thou hast said unto the LORD, Thou art my Lord: my goodness extendeth not to thee;
3 But to the saints that are in the earth, and to the excellent, in whom is all my delight.
4 Their sorrows shall be multiplied that hasten after another god: their drink offerings of blood will I not offer, nor take up their names into my lips.

5 The LORD is the portion of mine inheritance and of my cup: thou maintainest my lot.

6 The lines are fallen unto me in pleasant places; yea, I have a goodly heritage.

7 I will bless the LORD, who hath given me counsel: my reins also instruct me in the night seasons.

8 I have set the LORD always before me: because he is at my right hand, I shall not be moved.

9 Therefore my heart is glad, and my glory rejoiceth: my flesh also shall rest in hope.

10 For thou wilt not leave my soul in hell; neither wilt thou suffer thine Holy One to see corruption.

11 Thou wilt shew me the path of life: in thy presence is fulness of joy; at thy right hand there are pleasures for evermore.

About the Author

ROSANNA CEREZO SHARPS enjoys sharing God's Word to better understand and develop our relationship with the Heavenly Father, and to provide directives for life's challenges through its application. By vicariously experiencing another person's difficulties as they strive to maintain their course on the "narrow path"† to God, one can summarize his or her spiritual journey. Realizing "there is nothing new under the sun"*, she hopes to convey a picture of this process through the character's lives in her historical fiction trilogy *Golden Harvest*. The author prayerfully crafted the story, which allegorically applies to the timeless parables and other scriptural passages found in the Bible to help enlighten the pathway for God's people.

Rosanna studied Psychology at Southwestern College and theology at Calvary Chapel Bible College. She taught Bible studies for women, youth, and grade school children at several Calvary Chapel churches, including the church her husband pastored in Rio Vista, California. They have a musically gifted son whom she homeschooled. Her passion is to study God's Word and pray, to love her family, writing, fellowship with other Believers, singing worship songs, reenacting historical periods, travel and enjoying God's creation, and being creative through crafts such as crocheting, knitting, and painting. Currently, she and her husband are sole proprietors of a book and variety store in the historic town, Columbia, California, where all her attributes can be utilized by God to creatively plant the seed of His gospel to peoples around the globe.

† Matthew 7:13-14
* Ecclesiastes 1:9

Wheat Harvestor, Merced County

Harvesting Wheat, Merced County

Farm Hands baling hay, Tuolumne County

Farm hands preparing a load, Tuolumne County

Livestock barn, Tuolumne County

A typical ranch or farm home. Ralph's Ranch in Sonora.

A large ranch or farm estate in Snelling

Chinese Farm Hand, Tuolumne County

Chinese Cook, Tuolumne County

Portrait of Chinese Woman, Tuolumne County

Preparing a load to take to the flour mill, Tuolumne County

A Cargo Hauler taking lumber to the mill, Tuolumne County

Lumber Mill at Merced Falls Dam

Nelson's Woolen and Flour Mill at Merced Falls

Henry Nelson's Farm House

STAGING TO SONORA, CAL TWENTY FIVE YEARS AGO

Taking the stage to Sonora

Stage Line on Millerton Road

A typical livery and stable, Tuolumne County

Festivities in Snelling. Picture taken from Snelling Courthouse second floor steps. Snelling Hotel and the "Brave Old Oak" in the background.

www.ingramcontent.com/pod-product-compliance
Lightning Source LLC
Chambersburg PA
CBHW022042240626
47154CB00007B/2526